I could see their feet now through Suzie's legs. Sports socks. Trainers. Warren Spigott's black boots.

For a second, nothing happened. Then Warren said something that turned me to ice. 'Hey, hold up. Do you *know* this toad?'

'Who?' barked Gemma.

'*Darryl Otterwell.*'

My heart thumped. I wanted to be sick . . . 'Give Otterwell a message from me,' said Warren. 'Tell him, Warren says, *"It isn't over".*'

There was a sudden heavy clatter of plastic. Something had been thrown into the wheelie bin. The lid had been lifted and dropped so quickly that Garry, thankfully, hadn't been detected. Warren and his mates drifted off up the road.

What seemed like an age went by, then Suzie gave the all-clear.

Garry popped up like a jack-in-the-box. He was flustered and sweating and he smelt disgusting. There was sauce on his nose, chip ends in his hair and mushy pea stains down the front of his shirt. But that wasn't all. He'd come out clutching a torn-up workbook.

'It's yours,' he said, handing me the shreds . . .

www.**books**at**transworld**.co.uk/childrens

Also available by Chris d'Lacey,
and published by Corgi Books:

FLY, CHEROKEE, FLY
Highly Commended for the Carnegie Medal

Published by Corgi Yearling Books:

RIVERSIDE UNITED!

SCUPPER HARGREAVES:
FOOTBALL GENIE

CHRIS d'LACEY

PAWNEE WARRIOR

CORGI BOOKS

PAWNEE WARRIOR
A CORGI BOOK : 0 552 547883

First publication in Great Britain

PRINTING HISTORY
Corgi edition published 2002

1 3 5 7 9 10 8 6 4 2

Set in 12/15.5pt Palatino by
Phoenix Typesetting, Ilkley, West Yorkshire

Corgi Books are published by Transworld Publishers,
61–63 Uxbridge Road, London W5 5SA,
a division of The Random House Group Ltd,
in Australia by Random House Australia (Pty) Ltd,
20 Alfred Street, Milsons Point, Sydney, NSW 2061, Australia,
in New Zealand by Random House New Zealand Ltd,
18 Poland Road, Glenfield, Auckland 10, New Zealand
and in South Africa by Random House (Pty) Ltd,
Endulini, 5a Jubilee Road, Parktown 2193, South Africa

Made and printed in Great Britain by
Cox & Wyman Ltd, Reading, Berkshire

For Sue – who else?

I would like to express my thanks to:

David Glover for his help and advice on all aspects of pigeon racing;
Jim Wilson for showing me around his loft;
and Amy, who knows a lot more about genetics than I do.

CHAPTER ONE

'*Genetics*,' Mr Preston boomed. 'What is it? What's it all about? What importance does it have in all our lives?' He chalked the word up on the board. 'Darryl? What do you think?'

I picked up my pen and started doodling on my workbook. 'Dunno, sir. Sorry.'

'Well, would you like to hazard a *guess*?'

I blanked him out.

'Obviously not. Anyone?'

Suzie McAllister, the new girl, raised her hand. 'Sir, is genetics that thing where you can tell what someone is going to look like because their parents looked like them already?'

My best mate, Garry Taylor, nudged me in the ribs. 'What's she on about?' he hissed.

I shrugged. I didn't care. In another ten

minutes the bell would ring and I'd be on my way home to see if—

'Darryl, don't slouch,' Mr Preston said. 'Stop scribbling and pay attention.' He pushed his glasses to the top of his nose. 'Yes, Susan. Genetics is the basic science of heredity, the means by which we might expect to determine the characteristics of our offspring.'

'Our *what*?' said Connor Dorley.

'Babies, stupid,' Gemma Thomson drawled, giving Connor a dumb-mouthed stare.

'Aw, not *babies*,' Ryan Harvey muttered.

'That'll do,' Mr Preston warned. He went on the search for a new piece of chalk.

Garry seized the chance to glance at my workbook. 'What you writing?'

'Nothing.'

'Show us.'

'Bog off.'

'Face the board, please,' Mr Preston said, drawing two stick figures side by side. He labelled one MR BLOGGS, the other MRS BLOGGS. Then he drew a smaller figure below the main two. He labelled that one BABY BLOGGS.

'What colour are Mister's eyes?' he asked.

'White,' said Gazza. 'And his nose. And his gob.'

A few people sniggered.

Mr Preston rubbed out Mr Bloggs' eyes. 'Come on: a colour.'

'Blue,' said Fern Summers.

'Thank you.' Mr Preston squiggled them in blue. 'And Mrs B?'

'Hazel,' said Gemma. 'Like mine, sir.' She pushed her blonde curls off her brow, simpered like a model and fluttered her lashes.

Gazza made a vomiting noise.

Mr Preston gave Mrs Bloggs brownish-coloured eyes. 'Right, here we have one parent with blue eyes; the other with "hazel". Question: given this mix, what colour would we expect their *child's* eyes to be?' As he said this he drifted across to the windows, drawn by someone shouting in the playground.

Gazza grabbed the chance to pester me again. 'It's eighteen days today, isn't it?'

A chill ran up my spine. 'So?' I said, scowling. 'Nothing's gonna *happen.*'

'Come on,' said Mr Preston. 'Someone have a stab at it.'

'Can I come for tea at your house tonight?'

I shuddered and my pencil hit the floor.

'I'll help with the pigeons.'

'*No!* You can't!'

Gemma Thomson, with one eye on us and the other on the teacher, tapped an urgent alarm.

9

Too late: Mr Preston had heard me squawk. 'Can't what?' he snapped, jutting out his chin. 'Stand up, the pair of you. What's so fascinating that it simply can't wait until the bell?'

We pushed back our chairs and stood. I thought I heard something drop to the floor, but now wasn't the time to look.

Garry bit his lip. 'Sir, we were talking about . . . pigeons, sir.'

My heart thumped.

'*Pigeons?*' Gemma Thomson sneered.

'Be quiet,' said Mr Preston. 'Well, come on, enlighten me.'

Garry shifted his feet. 'We were wondering, sir, what colour pigeon you'd get if a black and white one had babies with a sort of reddy-grey one.'

I looked down at my feet and wanted to shrivel. Why was Garry *saying* this? He knew what had happened after—

Once again, Mr Preston broke my thoughts. 'You know, I'd really like to believe you, Garry. If I thought for one moment that—'

'Sir – Darryl keeps pigeons, sir.'

Mr Preston let out a sigh. 'Thank you, Connor. I am *aware* of Darryl's avian interests.' He renewed his stare, but now a thoughtful look had crept onto his face. 'Very well, Garry, as you were the one who posed the question, why don't you take a stab at the answer? What sort of markings do you think you'd see if you crossed a reddish-coloured bird with a mottled black and white one? For black, I would actually read "dark blue".'

Garry picked at his nails. 'Red and blue?' he guessed.

The class exploded with laughter.

Mr Preston waited for silence. 'And why do you say that?'

Garry shrugged. 'It's a sort of mixture, I s'pose.'

'You wouldn't say that one colour was more common in pigeons than any other?'

'They're usually grey,' said Fern.

Mr Preston raised a hopeful eyebrow. 'And why do you think that is . . . anyone?'

Before 'anyone' could answer, Suzie asked, 'Are Darryl's pigeons going to have babies, sir?'

Then the bell went.

'WAIT!' Mr Preston boomed. He trained his eye on the two of us again. 'As you pair saw fit to interrupt my lesson, I'm going to ask you to carry out a little experiment. I take it your birds *have* laid eggs, Darryl?'

'Yes, sir. But—'

'Good. In that case, when the eggs have

hatched I want you to observe the young and make notes of their changes over the next few weeks. Don't tell us what colour feathers they produce – I want everyone to guess. We'll have a competition. Tonight's homework: write in your workbooks what colour you think the baby pigeons will be, and why.'

Everyone groaned.

'Remember the cross: the father is . . . the red one, Darryl?'

I nodded.

'And the mother is bluey-black with white patches. There will be a *prize*, of course. I'll decide later what it is. Right, off you go.'

The stampede began.

I looked hard at Gazza. He was biting his lip.

Through the scrape of chairs I heard Suzie ask, 'Darryl, when will the babies hatch?'

But I'd snatched up my bag and was heading for the cloakroom.

Forgetting to look for whatever it was I'd dropped on the floor.

CHAPTER TWO

I argued with Garry all the way home. I asked him why he'd said what he had about the pigeons when he knew that certain . . . *things* couldn't happen.

'Got us sorted with Preston,' he sniffed. 'We could always make it up about the colours. We could say both babies came out grey.' His voice dropped. 'You know, if we had to.'

I stopped him at the gate. 'What do you mean, if we *had to*? They're s'posed to be sitting on *plastic* eggs!'

He blushed like mad and rolled a pebble underfoot. Then suddenly he frowned and turned the tables. 'What do you mean, *s'posed* to be sitting on plastic eggs?'

Then it was my cheeks burning.

Thankfully, Mum appeared on the drive,

bringing out some stuff for the bin. She spotted Garry and her eyes rolled skywards. She didn't bother asking if he'd like to stay for tea. Gazza was *always* round. Mum said he had a season ticket to our kitchen. 'What are you pair looking so secretive about?' She emptied the rubbish with a sturdy shake.

'Nothing,' we gulped.

Mum hummed and said, 'Well, behave your-selves, we've got a visitor: your Grandma Thornton's here, Darryl.'

'Ace,' I said, and hurried inside.

Grandma was sitting on a chair by the fridge, bouncing my little sister Natalie on her lap. 'Hi, Gran.' I ran up and kissed her cheek.

'Hello, pet.'

'This is Gazza, Gran.'

'A stray gannet we've taken to feeding,' said Mum, coming in and closing the door. She opened the freezer and took out a box of crispy cod fillets.

Grandma and Garry said hello.

'Gran, why are you here?' I asked. I shoved Garry onto another stool and took my favourite one by the window.

Gran bounced Natalie and made her giggle. 'Oh, just came to have a chat with your mum.'

Mum split a bag of oven chips and didn't say a word.

'How's that beautiful pigeon?'

My heart missed a beat. Garry jerked up as if he'd seen a ghost. What *was* the matter with him?

'I hear you got another one?' Gran continued.

'He's called Grepory Peg,' said Nat.

'Gregory Peck,' Mum corrected.

'I got him from Mr Duckins,' I said.

'Duckins?' Gran repeated, searching her memory. 'The pigeon fancier chap who helped you out with Cherokee?'

'Yes.'

'G'a'ma, Grepory made an egg!'

A tray of oven chips crashed to the floor. 'Oh, sausages!' went Mum, furious with herself.

'Sausages!' cried Natalie, clapping her hands.

Grandma looked at me and tilted her head. I crouched down and helped Mum gather up the chips.

'Goodness,' Gran said to Natalie. 'Gregory Peck's a clever pigeon if *he* can lay an egg.'

'Cherokee laid it – them,' I said.

'It would have been eighteen days, today,' said Gazza.

'Look,' said Mum, banging the flat of her hand on the worktop. 'Why don't you two buzz off

15

upstairs until tea's ready?' She turned and gave us a look.

Now what had got into *her*?

Then Natalie said: 'A girl came, G'a'ma. She put Grepory's eggs in the duzzbin.'

Mum sighed and turned to the window.

Grandma peered at me over her specs. So I told her the story. I began with the 'little accident', as Mum and Dad referred to it. How, eighteen nights ago, I'd found two eggs in Greg and Cherokee's nesting box.

'I see,' said Gran. 'And what did Dad have to say about that?'

Dad? He'd gone into orbit: *Eggs?! What do you mean, eggs? Now listen to me, Darryl. When your mother and I agreed to let you keep those pigeons, we did not expect a shed full by the summer! Those eggs have to go. Do I make myself clear?*

Crystal, *Dad*. But it wasn't *my* fault Greg and Cherokee had mated. When Mr Duckins gave me Greg he'd said there was no 'go' left in the bird. And although I could see Dad's point, I was wondering how the birds themselves would feel to come back and find their eggs removed. Which is why I'd called Mr Duckins for advice.

And he'd sent round his granddaughter, Susan.

She was older than me, by about two years. She had silky brown hair that bounced off her shoulders and big cow's eyes (so Mum said). When she looked at you you felt as if you ought to bow down. Garry hated her. I thought she was cool. She knew a lot about pigeons, and what to do with eggs.

'S'easy,' she'd said with a sniff. She'd reached into their box, through the hole in the cage front, lifted Greg off the nest and held him tight against her body. Then she'd dipped into the box again, removed the eggs and put them in my hands. Two warm white eggs, with two tiny lives growing inside them. Natalie had stood on tiptoes to see. Mum folded her arms and looked away. Dad just frowned and rubbed his lip.

Susan put her hand into the pocket of her blazer. She was still wearing her red school uniform. She produced more eggs. Only these didn't have any life inside them. They were made of plastic.

She dropped them into the nest. They rolled together with a gentle clack. Then she set Greg back on the perch of the nesting box and let him climb inside again. He nudged the dummy eggs once or twice with his beak, then settled on the nest as if nothing had happened.

'They'll sit them out for a bit,' said Susan. 'Then give up and start again.' And she'd dusted down her skirt as if she'd done nothing more than take a couple of apples from a fruit bowl.

'What about these?' I'd cupped the real eggs in my palm.

Susan looked at me as if I was thick. 'You ditch them, stupid.' And she'd taken them from me and done just that: put them in the dustbin and clamped down the lid.

'Goodness,' said Gran, having heard enough. 'She sounds like a girl who knows her own mind.'

'She's mardy,' sniffed Garry.

'No, she isn't,' I said hotly.

Mum and Gran exchanged a look. 'Brazen little madam,' Mum said dismissively. 'All lips and hair and "look at me" stances.'

'She know a lot about birds,' I said.

'And bees, I bet,' Mum put in.

'Bees?' said Garry, looking puzzled.

Grandma laughed and quickly announced: 'I would like to see Gregory Peck.'

Natalie let out an excited gasp. 'I'll show you, G'a'ma!' She slid off Gran's knee and scooted to the door.

'Nat!' I snapped. 'Don't you dare go in the shed!'

But by the time I'd made it onto the patio, she was already lifting the latch. She yanked the door open. 'Grepory!'

With a clatter of wings, Cherokee Wonder, my hen, fluttered out. She touched her pale pink feet to the lawn, then took off for the drainpipe beneath the bathroom window where she and Greg liked to perch in the sun.

'That's Cherokee,' said Garry, stepping out with Gran.

'Yes, I've seen her before,' she said.

'*Here*, G'a'ma!' Natalie shouted. She pointed at the shed and stomped inside.

I dived in after her. Greg wooed with alarm at the sight of a bouncy five-year-old and leapt onto the perch of the nesting box. I grabbed Nat by the collar and dragged her away, just as Greg spread his wings and flew.

Natalie squealed and stamped her feet. The clatter reverberated round the wooden panels. Silence descended. I looked anxiously into the box.

In the centre of the nest were two white eggs. One was slightly marked with pigeon poo. It lay in the corner, snug and still.

The second egg was rocking from side to side. There was a perfect circular split all around it.

Suddenly, the cap of the egg fell away.

And out of the shell poked a tiny pink head.

CHAPTER THREE

'This is a cosy roost,' said Gran. 'Was that Gregory that just flapped out?'

I couldn't speak. I was frozen, watching the newborn chick. Its head was swaying back and forth as if someone was trying to charm it with a flute. Its face was pink. Its beak was black. Wisps of downy yellow hair were curling over its wrinkled body. Its large, bald eyelids were firmly closed.

I had a baby pigeon.

'Darryl, love? What's the matter?' Grandma again, sounding concerned.

Garry pushed his way in. He sucked in sharply when he saw the chick.

Then, outside, I heard a voice call, 'Hello?' Dad. Home from work already.

Now the trouble was really going to start.

'Hello, Tim,' said Gran, backing out into the garden. They greeted with a gentle hug.

'Welcome to the pigeon loft,' said Dad. There was laughter in his voice. He was in a good mood. He wouldn't be laughing soon.

'What you gonna do?' Gazza gave me a nudge.

I shook my head, too scared to speak.

'We could smuggle it out in a plant pot,' he said.

I shook my head again. 'Dad's gonna go mental.'

Garry glanced outside. 'Shut up, he'll hear you.'

As it happened, Dad didn't. But Grandma did.

'What are you doing here?' I heard Dad ask her.

She patted his arm and stepped back inside the shed. 'Tell you in a minute.' Waving Garry aside, she peered into the nest box. Her face creased in gentle surprise. She slid a supportive arm around my shoulder. 'Lovely, aren't they? Squabs, I mean? When your Grandad Thornton was keeping pigeons, the birth of a squab always made him very happy. Later, when it finds its voice and starts calling for food, it becomes a squeaker. Then you'll know it's around, all right.'

'Dad's gonna kill me, Gran.'

She drew me in close. 'No, he isn't.' She led me out into the light.

'Darryl, what's the matter?' Dad saw right away that something was up.

'You have a new arrival in the family,' said Gran.

'New arrival?' Dad sounded confused.

'It's my fault,' said Garry.

'Shut up,' I told him.

'G'a'ma, there's Grepory Peg,' said Nat. She pointed to the roof of the shed. Greg scrabbled down the felt and hopped onto the top of the open door. Edging sideways and tilting forward, he peered into the shed to check it was safe, then fluttered back to his nesting box.

'Gone to look after his young,' said Gran.

'His *what*?' There was ice in Dad's voice now.

'It's my fault,' said Garry.

'Shut *up!*' I growled.

'Darryl, what's going on?' asked Dad.

Grandma gave my shoulders a squeeze. 'Gregory Peck and Cherokee Wonder have hatched a chick.'

Dad's face turned grey, then pink, then purple. 'But that's impossible. They're sitting on plastic eggs. What are you playing at, Darryl? Have you arranged some plan with that Duckins girl?'

'No!' I shouted. 'It's not her fault.'

'It's *my* fault,' said Garry. And this time, he wouldn't can it. 'I took the real eggs out of the dustbin and swapped them for the plastic ones.'

'You did *what*?' Dad pulled back his jacket like a gunfighter getting ready to draw.

'He's lying,' I shouted. 'He didn't do it, Dad.'

'Yes I did,' said Garry.

'No, you *didn't*,' I said, gritting my teeth. I was thinking I was going to have to smack him in a minute.

Gazza went red and shoved his hands into his pockets. 'Yes I *did*,' he insisted.

Dad spread his hands. 'What the *hell* is going on?'

Grandma called for calm. She turned to Garry. 'Are you trying to protect Darryl, Garry?'

'No,' he said bluntly. 'I really did swap them.'

'But you couldn't have,' I railed. '*I* swapped them! Straight after Susan had gone. I sneaked out and took the real eggs from the dustbin, then I put them back in the nest.'

Garry suddenly looked very foolish. 'You mean, when I did it after tea, I put the *plastic* ones back?'

Grandma's eyebrows raised a little higher.

'Oh, this is ridiculous,' said Dad. 'If Darryl

switched them first and then Garry put the plastic eggs back in the nest, how the heck have we got a baby pigeon?!'

'Well, it's obvious,' said Gran, picking a piece of cotton off Dad's lapel. 'Someone must have switched them again.'

'Well I know it wasn't me,' Dad snapped. 'And Natalie wouldn't do it. So who else?'

'It was me.'

We all turned together. Mum was there, with a tear on her cheek and a hand on her tummy.

'Claire?' said Dad, not sure whether to be angry or confused.

'Sorry, Tim. I just couldn't bear it. Not in my present condition.'

Dad gulped and looked at the hand on her tummy.

Mum nodded. 'I'm pregnant,' she said.

CHAPTER FOUR

'I thought she was looking fat,' Garry whispered. The remark was meant for my ears only, but Mum homed in on it right away.

'I heard that, you cheeky monkey! It's only three months. I'm not even showing!'

'Three *months*?' Dad ran a hand down her arm.

Mum sniffed and pulled a tissue from her sleeve.

'Boys, how about you pop round to the chip shop and buy us all supper?' Gran opened her purse and handed me a couple of ten-pound notes.

'Smart,' said Garry. 'Can I have ginger beer?'

'Have what you like,' Grandma told him, steering us away from Mum and Dad.

I looked over my shoulder as we headed for the house. Mum and Dad were in a clinch.

25

Dad was looking up at the sky, running his knuckles along her back. 'Is Mum all right?' I asked.

'She is now,' said Gran. Then the doorbell rang. She looked up and frowned. 'Whoever that is, tell them to come back later.'

'Gran, what about . . . ?' I glanced at the shed.

'After tea,' she said. 'Go on, off you go. And don't put any salt on my chips.'

We hurried through the house and opened the door. Gemma Thomson was on the step.

'Come back later,' Garry said immediately.

'Bog off, Taylor.' Gemma shoved a sweet lollipop into her mouth and twiddled the short white stick with her fingers. She looked me up and down. 'Hi, Darryl.'

'What do you want?' I asked, my tone only slightly less blunt than Garry's.

Gemma swung her hips. She had her left arm tucked up behind her back. 'Nothing. Just passing.'

'Why'd you ring the bell, then?' Gazza snorted.

'To see if you'd come to the door, *idiot*.'

'You're mental,' he said, barging past.

She whacked his arm with a flat, green book. It looked like her workbook from Mr Preston's class.

'We're going to the chip shop,' I said. I pulled the door to and trudged after Garry.

'That's cool,' Gemma said, and quickly made a beckoning motion with her hand.

Across the road, Suzie McAllister and Fern Summers were sitting on a low wall, swinging their legs. They went into a huddle when they saw we'd clocked them. I saw Suzie shake her head. Her long hair danced. Fern pulled her quickly to her feet.

We headed down the hill towards the shops, Gemma skipping along like a kid behind us.

'Get lost,' said Garry, unnerved by her nearness.

'Free world,' she sniffed, rolling her lollipop across her mouth. 'Suzie wants to know about your pigeons, Darryl.'

I glanced back at Suzie. She blushed and looked away.

'She wasn't here last term when you did your project.' She patted the workbook against her thigh.

'Why are you carrying your workbook?' I asked.

Fern snickered. Suzie turned. The others tugged her back.

'She wants to know if your pigeons are *really* having babies.'

27

'They've just *had* one,' said Gazza, walking backwards a bit.

That made me think about Mum. Was I really going to have another sister – or brother? The thought was weird. It made me shudder.

'Ace,' said Gemma. 'Tell us what colour. Then we can win Preston's stupid competition.'

'Yellow,' Gazza answered.

'He's lying,' scoffed Fern.

''Tis,' said Gazza. 'Dead ugly, too.'

'Well, *you'd* know, wouldn't you?' Gemma sneered.

Gazza went for her then. She squealed and took refuge behind a pillar box.

Suzie stepped to one side, out of the ruck. 'I expect it won't get its proper colours till it grows a bit older, will it?'

I looked at her again. She pulled up a sock.

'What you gonna call it?' Fern piped up. 'Is it gonna have an Indian name like . . . what's the other one called?'

'Cherokee.'

'Yeah.'

'We haven't decided,' said Gazza.

Excuse me? I thought. *They're my birds, Garry.*

'That's 'cos you don't know any,' Gemma taunted.

'Do!'

'Don't!'

'Tell us, then,' said Fern.

Garry clenched a fist. From deep within the recesses of a history lesson he managed to find a North American word: 'Tomahawk.'

'That's not a tribe name!' Gemma exploded. 'That's an axe!'

The girls collapsed with laughter. I shook my head in despair. Gazza was on his own with this. Besides, the chip shop was only round the corner. The smell of fried batter was in my nostrils. I pulled Gran's money from my pocket.

'It'd be an OK name for a *hawk*,' sneered Fern. 'He could call it Tommy for short.'

'I know some Indian names,' said Suzie. There was a helpful, apologetic tone in her voice, as if she was slightly ashamed of her mates. 'My dad's dead keen on Indians. He's got tons of books about them. I think Apache would be good.'

'For a patchy one, yeah!'

Yeah. Dead funny, Gemma. I wanted her to shut it – so I could hear Suzie out. At least she didn't talk rubbish all the time.

'Comanche,' she suggested. 'Or Hopi. Or Pawnee.'

'Poor knee?' queried Fern.

'They were dead brave – and fierce, I think.'

'Like Taylor's breath, you mean?' said Gemma.

'You're dead,' said Gazza and chased her round the corner.

Within ten seconds he was back, with a shaken, ashen look on his face. He stopped me only yards from the turn. 'We've gotta go,' he gulped.

My stomach tightened. 'Why?'

He dragged me to the corner, made me peek around the hedge.

I pulled back, panting.

Fern looked at me sideways, then peered round too. 'All I can see is some lads,' she reported.

Four lads. Four *big* lads. One of them had bullied me all last term and tried to steal Cherokee Wonder from me.

His name was Warren Spigott.

CHAPTER FIVE

'Are they after you?' asked Suzie, checking them out.

'That lad with the long black hair is,' said Gazza.

'The tasty one?' asked Fern, squeezing over Suzie's shoulder. 'Him in the cowboy boots? He's just sat down, flicking fizz at his mates.'

I squeezed my eyes shut and tried to breathe deeply.

Gemma reappeared then, looking confused. 'Thought you were getting chips?'

'Darryl's scared of those lads,' said Fern.

I started to turn.

'Wait,' said Suzie, holding me back. 'He can't do anything while we're here, can he?'

'He can,' said Gazza. 'That's Warren Spigott.

He's in Year Eleven. He's totally mental. He got suspended last term for picking on Darryl.'

Suzie paused a moment to take this in. 'Well, let's just wait here till they're gone.'

'I'll get the chips,' Gemma suggested. 'I'm not scared. They're only lads.' She whipped the money from my hand. 'What do you want?'

'Just chips,' said Gazza, 'for loads of people.'

'OK,' she peeped and disappeared round the corner.

Suzie McAllister pushed up her sleeves. I'd seen Mum do this when she was about to lecture me or take control of a difficult situation. Suzie was taking control. 'Fern, keep watching. If they come this way, squeal.'

'They're all on the bench now,' Fern reported. 'Except one with ginger hair. He's trying to stand a chip on the end of his nose. Gemma's gone in the shop.'

I slid to the pavement, sitting back against the hedge; Gazza did likewise, picking his nails. Suzie sat beside me, chewing her lip. Her long brown hair fell against my shoulder. She stretched out a leg and brushed some gravel off her skirt. 'What did he do to you, then?'

'It was all because of Cherokee,' Gazza blurted. 'Warren's dad, Lenny Spigott, is a top pigeon fancier. Cherokee used to belong to him.'

'Did you steal it?'

''Course not,' Gazza tutted.

'Long story,' I breathed, just as Fern flapped a hand.

'Hide! They're coming.'

I leapt to my feet.

'The wheelie!' said Gazza, pointing to a large black bin with two wheels at its base.

'You can't both hide behind that,' said Suzie.

Gazza weighed up the options. 'Darryl, jump in.'

'*What?*'

'Come on-nn,' Fern urged. 'They're razzing Gemma. Oh no, she's dropped the workbook!'

I couldn't understand what the workbook had to do with anything then. All I could think of was Warren's voice, shouting: 'Oi, mop-head. You dropped your *book*.'

'Give that back!' I heard Gemma snap.

'Gizz a kiss, first.'

'In your dreams!'

'*Woo-oo!*'

Gazza threw open the wheelie bin. 'If *you're* not getting in, I am.' He stepped up onto a low brick wall. With one quick leap, he was in.

Suzie dropped the lid. 'Darryl, get behind it. Me and Fern'll cover you.'

I dived behind the bin, just as Gemma came round the corner.

'Oh look, she's got a gang,' I heard Ginger sneer.

'Three of them, four of us. That's fair.'

'You leave us alone,' Suzie said calmly. 'I live round here. I'll shout my dad.'

'*I'll shout my dad,*' one of them parroted. I could see their feet now through Suzie's legs. Sports socks. Trainers. Warren Spigott's black boots.

For a second, nothing happened. Then Warren said something that turned me to ice. 'Hey, hold up. Do you *know* this toad?'

'Who?' barked Gemma.

'*Darryl Otterwell.*'

My heart thumped. I wanted to be sick. Warren hadn't seen me. If he had, I'd be dead. So what had made him mention my name?

'What if we do?' sniffed Gemma.

There was a slow, slow ripping sound.

'Oi!' went Fern. 'That doesn't belong to you!'

'Don't belong to him now, either,' said Warren. He tried to lamp Fern's ear. She squealed and ducked away. Suzie stretched her fingers and put a foot forward. For a moment, I thought she would take Warren on. But with Fern unhurt, she dropped back into line, keeping me undercover.

'Give Otterwell a message from me,' snarled Warren. 'Tell him, Warren says, "*It isn't over*".'

There was a sudden heavy clatter of plastic. Something had been thrown into the wheelie bin. The lid had been lifted and dropped so quickly that Garry, thankfully, hadn't been detected.

Warren and his mates drifted off up the road.

What seemed like an age went by, then Suzie gave the all-clear.

Garry popped up like a jack-in-the-box. He was flustered and sweating and he smelt disgusting. There was sauce on his nose, chip ends in his hair and mushy pea stains down the front of his shirt. But that wasn't all. He'd come out clutching a torn-up workbook. 'It's yours,' he said, handing me the shreds.

'We were bringing it to you,' Gemma said quietly. 'You dropped it in class.' She glanced at Suzie, who looked away fast.

I opened the first few pages. All my science work, torn to bits. Preston was going to explode. I sighed and looked at the cover. My name had been ripped in three distinct places. Only one word had survived the attack. It was written across a corner in flowing, curved letters. The doodle I hadn't dared show to Gazza. One single name, surrounded by hearts.

SUSAN.

CHAPTER SIX

That night I sat on the garden bench for ages. I should have been looking after the birds, scraping their droppings off the floor of the shed, changing the water in their drinker, putting fresh mix in the feeding hopper. But I couldn't find the will to do it. Warren Spigott's threat was like a rope around my ankles.

Tell him, it isn't over.

Around half past six Mum came out. She sat down beside me with her hands on her thighs, as if we were strangers on a railway platform. 'Look at him, wrecking my greenery again.'

Greg was perched on the rim of a planter, tugging at a purple clematis. With a fierce nip he broke a piece off. The stem flipped comically out of his beak. He twisted his neck to see where it had fallen, then fluttered to the ground to retrieve it. After several attempts he pecked up the piece, twiddled it in his beak, dropped it again, repeated the procedure until the stem was correctly aligned, then flew into the shed with it. 'Lining his nest,' said Mum.

'Do you want me to put him in?'

She shook her head. 'Flowers are nearly over, anyway.' She reached out then and took my hand. She placed it in her lap and rubbed it gently. 'There's something I want to tell you, Darryl. Something important – about the baby.'

I glanced at her waist. She was wearing slacks and a loose-fitting sweater. Not bulging at all.

She squeezed my hand. 'Your dad and I hadn't planned to tell you this – not until you were older at any rate. But under the present circumstances, I think it's only fair you should know.' She paused and took a breath. 'Altogether, I've been pregnant five times in my life. The first time was two years before you were born; the third occasion was between you and Natalie; the fifth is now.' She tightened her lip and stared straight ahead. 'In other words, I've had two babies, and I've lost two babies. The ones I lost both died, in here.' She patted her tummy. 'Do you understand?'

Up the garden Greg fluttered back to the shed.

He wooed with pride as he delivered his latest addition to the nest.

I nodded.

'After Natalie,' Mum went on, 'the doctors advised us not to try again for any more children.' She paused and ran a knuckle under her eye. 'This baby wasn't planned. It came about . . . Well, it doesn't matter how it came about; what's done is done. What *does* matter is that we all try to pull together as a family. Things are going to be a bit . . . topsy-turvy. Grandma's going to move in for a while, just to help out around the house.'

I went tight inside then and stared at the ground. I knew what it really meant, Grandma moving in. It was in case . . . 'Why did the other babies die?' I asked.

Mum raised her chin. She pulled a strand of hair from the corner of her mouth. I realized then that she'd been crying gently, talking normally through the tears. 'It's not very easy to explain,' she answered. 'It's just something that runs in the family. A sort of hereditary thing.'

'Genetics?'

She gave me a studious look. 'Hmm. I didn't know you knew about things like that?'

I told her about Mr Preston's homework.

She smiled and cast her gaze at Greg. He was

strutting through the border plants, pecking for grit. 'Your dad's not happy about those eggs. The timing's a bit . . . unfortunate, really. The best you can do is try to lie low and make sure the birds are properly looked after. You ought to find out if there's anything special that needs to be done.'

'I'll ring Mr Duckins.'

'I thought Mr Duckins had stopped keeping birds?'

'He still knows what to do.' At least *Susan* did. I thought about her then. Her big, brown eyes. How she tilted her head to play with her hair. That thing she did with her heel on the ground, swinging her foot from side to side. 'I'll go and ring him now,' I said.

'Darryl?' Mum sighed and released my hand. 'I know Mr Duckins is an expert on pigeons, but he wasn't in good health the last I heard. You really mustn't pester him. What about that other chap, Mr Spigott? The one who owned Cherokee before you found her? Didn't he say you could give him a call if you ever needed advice about the birds?'

'I've got to go and clean the shed,' I said, and hurried away with my heart thumping. Call Lenny Spigott? And risk getting *Warren*?

I'd rather jump into a crocodile pool.

'Darryl?' Mum called. But I didn't want to know.

I was ringing Mr Duckins.

And that was that.

CHAPTER SEVEN

'*Hatched?!*' Susan Duckins' shriek of disbelief could have been heard in another county. 'How?'

Telling her was harder than telling Dad.

'You're cracked,' she came back. 'What you gonna do?'

'Don't know,' I said meekly. 'Do you wanna come and see it?'

'It?' Her voice went up another tone.

'The second one hasn't come out yet.'

She sighed heavily and muttered, 'Pathetic . . .'

'I just want someone to check they're all right.'

'I'm not a *vet*, Darryl!'

'But you're dead good with pigeons.'

The flattery seemed to work the magic. 'It'll have to be Sunday. I'm busy till then.'

'Thanks,' I said.

'You're cracked,' she reminded me, and banged the phone down.

She turned up just before tea. She was wearing jeans and a baggy blue top, her hair held back with an orange grip. She had studs in her ears, gum in her mouth, a chain of pale blue stars round her neck. It was the first time I'd seen her out of her uniform. She looked . . . awesome.

She propped her bike up against Dad's car. When he told her to shift it, she huffed and wheeled it into the garden. Natalie was there, playing on her swing. Susan glared at her. Natalie spooked. She hooked a finger in her mouth and ran to the kitchen. I saw Grandma standing at the kitchen window, tending the leaves of a spider plant. I knew she was spying. So was Mum. Eyes followed Susan everywhere.

Susan, indifferent to the fuss she was causing, marched boldly into the shed. It was Greg's turn to sit the young. She parted his breast feathers and inspected the squabs, as if she needed to see the evidence before she'd truly believe the madness.

'The other one came out yesterday,' I said.

My proud smile made her roll her eyes. She pulled a sachet of something out of her pocket.

The end had been torn and taped back down. 'Put this in their water, every day. Instructions are on the packet. Grandad says it helps with feather growth. You haven't got a nest bowl, so you're gonna have to clean round those twigs every day. You'll get flies and stuff if it gets too yucky. Then the squabs might get diseases.'

'How long will it take them to grow?' I asked. 'Into proper pigeons?'

'Fledglings,' she tutted; 'they're already pigeons. They'll start their pin feathers soon. Takes about a month till they're properly covered. What you gonna do when they have feathered up?'

I shrugged. 'Depends on Dad. He's mad at me for letting them hatch. I want to race them. That'd be cool.'

'How?' she sneered. 'You're not in a club.'

'I know. Do you think you grandad will help me?'

A cold breeze whistled through the knots in the panelling. 'Grandad's sick. He's got a chest infection. He might have to go to hospital.'

I wanted to say I was sorry to hear that. Alf Duckins had been really good to me once. He'd given me Gregory Peck, after all. But Susan, tired for the moment of talking, marched out of the shed without another word.

By now Mum and Gran were in the garden, taking in a line of washing. Dad was out too, chatting quietly to Mum. She waved him to be quiet when she saw us coming and clamped a few pegs between her teeth.

'All sorted?' asked Gran, catching Susan's eye.

'Good as it can be,' Susan sniffed.

Mum's gaze was like a laser, wanting to frazzle her.

Gran said, 'Darryl, have you asked Susan if she'd like to stay for tea?'

Mum spat a peg across the lawn.

'Can't,' said Susan. 'Gotta be somewhere.'

'Well, another time, perhaps. How are Pawnee and Sioux?'

Susan stopped in her tracks. 'Who?'

'Hasn't Darryl told you their names? We had a lovely time deciding them last night. Pawnee Warrior for the cock; Suzie Sioux for the hen.'

Suzie's namesake wrinkled her nose.

'Darryl's mum likes the name Susan,' said Gran.

'She used to,' Mum muttered.

Susan pulled off her grip and flicked out her hair. 'I think it's a rubbish name.'

'I like it,' I said.

'You would, you're a lad.'

'Well, thank goodness for *that*,' growled Mum.

Susan glared at her hard. Mum pointed at the sky. 'Got the washing in before it rained.' She threw a peg into the basket and marched down the path.

Susan stared after her a moment, and yawned. 'Oh, I forgot to tell you, Darryl. If you're gonna race *Pawnee and Sioux*, you're gonna have to ring them soon. If you leave it too long their legs grow too thick. Then you can't put a ring on.'

Dad's gaze slid towards me like a rifle sight.

'Gotta go,' said Susan, sensing tension. She plucked a feather off her arm and blew it in my face.

'Darryl, walk Susan to her bike,' said Gran.

'I'm not a crock,' said Susan.

Gran gave her a look. 'Darryl's being brought up to be polite. Have a safe journey home.'

Susan twitched an eyebrow and turned away.

As I walked her back to the gate, Gran fell into a whispered conversation with Dad. I had the feeling it must be to do with the pigeons. Gran was on my side. She always was. Maybe she'd persuade him to let me race them?

Maybe.

'See you, then.' Susan clicked the latch on the gate.

'Thanks for coming,' I said, returning to the moment.

46

She swept back her hair, clearing her cheek. My stomach tightened. Was she expecting me to kiss her goodbye?

If she was, I waited a second too long. 'I'm off,' she said pertly. 'Your mum's watching.'

I turned to the kitchen.

When I turned back the gate was closed, and Susan and my chances of a kiss had gone.

CHAPTER EIGHT

I replayed that moment over and over. Sometimes it worked out just the way it was: I turned, she went, I beat the air in frustration. Other times I'd give her a clumsy peck and she'd snap, 'What you doing?' and I'd blush into my socks. Sometimes, she gave *me* a peck and my body tightened up like a wound propellor. But the best were those dreams where I kissed her softly and she chewed her lip and could barely whisper, 'Bye.' Those left me tingling inside.

I was wandering along the science block corridor, lost in one of those tingling moments, when Garry broke my daydream as only Garry could.

'WHAT?! NO CHANCE!'

'Is there a fire, Mr Taylor?' Mr Preston swept by me, carrying a model of the circulatory system.

Garry shook his head.

'An unexpected volcanic eruption?'

'No, Mr Preston.'

'Alien spaceship on the horizon?'

Gazza looked out of the window to be sure. 'No, sir.'

'Then don't SHOUT!' The force of the reprimand lifted Garry's fringe.

Mr Preston backed into the classroom, holding his plastic lungs to his chest.

Gazza waited till he'd gone, then said, 'Bog off, Thomson. You're seriously weird.'

Gemma cocked a hip. She'd cornered Garry up against the lockers. Suzie and Fern were hovering nearby.

'Tell Darryl,' said Fern, seeing me approach.

'Tell me what?' I said.

Gemma looked me up and down. 'We're gonna be your angels.'

Suzie sighed and picked some paint off a window catch.

'We're gonna protect you from Warren,' said Fern.

'Like angels,' said Gemma. 'We're gonna watch over you.'

I looked at Gazza. We started for the classroom.

'Wait.' Gemma tugged my arm. 'All we're

gonna do is hang around with you.'

'Get lost,' I tutted. Hang around with *girls*? Me and Gazza? No way.

'Warren can't get you if *we're* there,' Fern argued. 'Anyway, we've got a secret weapon.' She prodded Suzie. Suzie batted her off.

'Careful, she's dangerous,' Gemma sniffed.

'Suzie does judo,' Fern said proudly. 'Her dad's a fitness instructor.'

'She's got belts,' said Gemma. 'Haven't you, Suze?'

Suzie folded her arms. The windows reflected her deep dark frown. 'Fighting isn't right,' she muttered.

Gemma, as usual, overruled her. 'If you fight her, she'll chuck you.'

'Sure,' said Gazza.

'Try it, *big mouth*.'

'Gem! Pack it in!' Suzie's chestnut-coloured eyes were blazing. She pointed a toe and tapped the floor hard. If she and Gemma got into a scrap, I knew which one I'd back.

'I'm only trying to *show* them,' Gemma hissed, all hands and sighs and in-your-face looks. 'It was *you* who said Darryl shouldn't get bullied.'

The bell went for Preston's lesson. Suzie whirled on her heels, stomped into the classroom and slammed her bag down. Gemma caught me watching her and said, very quietly, 'Dead nice, isn't she, Darryl?'

I hitched my bag onto my shoulder. 'I don't want protecting, *thanks*.'

We hurried into class. Mr Preston closed the door. 'Right, workbooks out.'

My stomach knotted. Over the weekend I'd tried to put my mangled workbook back together. I'd patched it up with sticky tape and staples – but it still looked like first-aid for beginners.

'Don't dilly-dally,' Mr Preston barked, pounding the board with a duster. 'First, a quick update. Darryl, how are the pigeons? Stand up straight, so everyone can hear you.'

I hated doing this, spouting off to the class. It always made me feel like the last skittle in the alley. 'Both the eggs have hatched,' I muttered. 'One came out on Friday, after school. The other one cracked on Saturday afternoon.'

Mr Preston nodded. 'Yes, there's sometimes a delay before the second chick emerges. Anything else you can tell us?'

I described the squabs' appearance. Then Fern Summers stuck up her hand. 'Sir, has Darryl got names for them yet?'

Mr Preston used his eyebrows as a prompt.

I lifted a shoulder. 'The one that hatched first has got a small white blob on its beak—'

'Like Indian war paint,' Gazza chipped in.

'Smart,' said Connor, giving a thumbs-up sign.

'—I'm going to call that one Pawnee Warrior.'

That caused a rumble of voices.

Mr Preston shushed them. 'Good. And the second?'

I shifted my feet and squirmed a bit. I could already see Suzie McAllister looking a bit doe-eyed at me. 'Sioux,' I gulped.

Gemma's mouth fell open so wide you could have dropped a tennis ball in it with ease.

'Sioux? As in the Indian tribe?' said Mr Preston.

I nodded.

'Its proper name's Suzie Sioux,' said Garry.

There was a scrape of chairs as Fern and Gemma went into a huddle. Suzie seemed to have frozen to her seat.

'Yes, interesting choices,' Mr Preston said, smiling. 'Rather like these champion show dogs, isn't it? Periwinkle Powderpuff Snuggins and such.'

Ryan Harvey said, 'Whaaat?'

Mr Preston sighed. 'Oh, never mind. Right. Workbooks at the ready. I want you to—' He stopped mid-sentence, hands six inches from clapping together. He slid off his desk and came slowly down the classroom. He stopped by my desk and picked up my book. 'What's this?'

The room fell deathly quiet.

'Sir, my dog chewed it,' Gazza started up.

'Be quiet,' said Mr Preston, who could spot a fake excuse across a football pitch.

Gemma, 'my angel', attempted a rescue. 'Sir, it was my fault, really, sir. We were messing around on Great Elms Park and I got Darryl's workbook and chucked it on the grass, and the park keeper ran over it with his mower and—'

'Shut up, Gemma. I'm asking Darryl.'

But before I could speak, another voice cut in: 'Sir, I know what happened.'

Mr Preston switched his gaze to Suzie.

'Sir, we were near the park when these lads came up and grabbed Darryl's workbook and one of them ripped it.'

My body turned to stone. Gazza gasped in shock. Gemma and Fern could only gawp.

'Lads?' Mr Preston lifted his chin. I began to shake then. He was taking her seriously. His gaze fell on me. 'Is this right?'

Under the desk, I tightened my fists. Suzie McAllister was *dead*. 'Yes, sir.'

He nodded and steepled his fingers. 'Do you know these . . . lads?'

The burrowing gaze went back to Suzie. 'They were just some lads,' she muttered. Her hair fell across her face like a curtain.

Mr Preston pursed his lips. 'I see,' he whistled softly, and went to the cupboard. He skimmed a new workbook across my desk. 'Whatever you've lost I want copied out neatly. Get what you need from Garry. Tall task, Darryl. If I were you, I'd try to avoid these "lads" in future.'

'Yes, sir.' My cheeks were blistering with rage. Everyone except *McAllister the rat* was staring at me.

'Right, show's over,' Mr Preston barked. 'Now, let's get some learning done.'

CHAPTER NINE

I wanted to pull her stupid hair out. Strand by strand. Until she was bald. Gazza had a stronger suggestion than that. He said we should treat her like a real lab rat and put her in a cage and drip soap in her eyes like they did in . . . soap experiments.

In the end I drew a tombstone on the back of my workbook and wrote McRAT and the date on it. Gemma saw it and demanded an explanation. I said it meant Suzie 'didn't exist'. I never wanted to *see* her or *talk* to her or even be *near* her *ever* again.

Gemma said that was really mean, and she'd given Suzie a wagging, anyway. 'She skriked,' she said. 'She's really sorry. Don't bag her off, Darryl. She didn't mean any harm. You know you like her . . . *really*.'

'Get lost,' I said, and turned away.

'But what about—?'

'Just get lost, OK?'

'Lads!' she went. 'You're all so *fickle*!'

I hadn't got a clue what she meant.

I was still 'spitting feathers', as Gran would say, when I got home from school that night. There was no-one in the kitchen so I went to my room and flopped out, face down, on my bed.

I'd been lying no more than twenty seconds when I heard muffled voices from Mum and Dad's room. Suddenly, my name was mentioned. I rolled off the bed and crept to the landing.

I heard Mum say: 'You were the one who thought pigeons would be good for him.' Hangers swished across a wardrobe rail.

'This is different, Claire. This wasn't on the menu. We have to nip this thing in the bud, right now.'

'This "thing" means a lot to him,' Mum said bluntly. 'Why do you think he swapped those eggs? We taught him to respect life, not destroy it.'

There was a creak of boards as someone moved. 'We also tried to teach him that you have to be accountable for all your actions, especially the irresponsible ones.'

'Oh, and where does that leave me? I'm just as responsible as he is, remember? I'm accountable, too.'

I could picture Dad now running a hand through his hair, tightening his lip, looking down at his feet. 'We have to sort this, before it's out of control. It's too much, with the baby and everything.'

'Well, you've obviously made your mind up, so what's the point in—'

'Oh, don't be like that,' Dad cut across her sharply. 'I don't want him hurt, but something has to be done.'

There was another short pause. A drawer slammed shut. 'Look,' said Dad, 'I was talking to Annie in the garden yesterday. She's had a good idea, about the young birds.'

'I'm listening,' said Mum.

The door handle turned. I dived for my room. Not quickly enough.

'Darryl? Is that you?' Mum stepped onto the landing.

'Just come in, Mum.'

I glanced at Dad. He eyed me suspiciously. 'I'll talk to you later,' he said to

Mum. He touched her arm and went silently downstairs.

Next day at school I told Gazza what I'd heard. He said to ask Gran – in a secret sort of way. But Gran had gone back to Yorkshire for the day. I had no choice but to wait.

It didn't take long. Shortly after tea that night Dad called me into the hall. He handed me my coat. 'Put it on. We're going out.'

'Where?'

'You'll see.' There was tightness in his voice, but no real anger.

We got into the car and swept towards school. 'Am I in trouble?' I asked.

We flashed past the park. 'No,' he said quietly, 'you're not in trouble.'

We passed the chip shop, the garage, the pub, the church. At the roundabout we didn't take the exit to school. We went west, out into open country, towards a village called Barrowmoor.

'I want to talk about the pigeons,' said Dad.

I looked through the window. Sheep were grazing in the open fields.

'I don't approve of what you did with those eggs.'

I folded my arms. 'It was Mum and Gazza, too.'

'That's no excuse. The intent was there. Anyway, what's done is done; we have to make the best of the situation now and— oh, we're here already.' He slowed the car down and took a right turn, into a winding, tree-lined avenue. 'Can you see the numbers on these houses at all?'

'Fourteen,' I said, reading a gate post.

He pulled up outside the next house along. Number 16 Station Road. 'Nice place,' he murmured. 'Not quite what I'd expected.'

We were in the middle of a new estate – a cluster of large, yellow-bricked houses with green-tiled roofs and dark brown doors. Circular rose-beds in tongue-shaped lawns. Why had he brought me here?

Somewhere up ahead, a brown door slammed. 'Come on,' said Dad. 'That might be him.'

We climbed out of the car as a figure came scuffing down the herring-bone drive. From the heaviness of step it sounded like a man. He was hidden for the moment by the branches of a tree. 'Hello,' said Dad. 'Is your father in?'

The approaching figure breathed out deeply. The smell of cigarette smoke filled the air. 'Out back, with his pigeons,' he sniffed.

The voice slammed me against the car.

'Darryl?' Dad turned and threw me a look.

'Darryl?' said the figure, and stepped into view.

Like a spider to a fly.

It was Warren Spigott.

CHAPTER TEN

'Darryl, what on earth's got into you? Don't slouch against the car. Stand up straight.' Dad gave me one of his frazzled looks, then turned to Warren Spigott and said, 'I'm Mr Otterwell. I rang last night. Your father's expecting us. It's to do with the pigeons, as a matter of fact.'

'Oh . . . right,' said Warren, taking this in. A cold smile played across his mouth. I could tell he'd been on edge for a moment, thinking this might be a confrontation. But with the mention of pigeons the threat had dissolved. 'Take you through then, shall I?' He dropped his cigarette and ground it with his heel.

'I think we can find our own way,' said Dad. Already there was quiet disapproval in his voice, his brow one line away from a scowl. He'd had enough time to rope Warren in and give him a mental 'dressing down', just like Mum had demolished Susan Duckins.

But Warren Spigott was used to demolition. He got it all the time at school. He swept back his hair, put a hand in his pocket and chewed an imaginary piece of gum. 'Best if we go through the garage,' he said.

Dad never found out it was Warren who had bullied me. When Warren was suspended from school, both sets of parents had been informed, but names had not been mentioned. Mr Blundell, the Head, had told me in his office: 'I am drafting letters to both sets of parents describing what has happened and what the school proposes to do. As a matter of principle, we will not be identifying each to the other. By that I mean that Warren Spigott will not be named as the bully to your parents. Similarly, you will not be identified as the victim in the letter being sent to his father. It is for you to decide whether you wish to inform your parents who the culprit was and how – or why – the bullying came about. Do you understand?'

Yes, Mr Blundell, I'd understood. But Mum and Dad hadn't. Mum had been visibly shocked by the letter. Dad had just gone ballistic. Four times he'd asked me who the boy was. But I wouldn't give a name. Couldn't give a name. I knew he'd find Warren, go round in a blaze and have him by the throat against a wall.

And now we *were* round. In Warren Spigott's garden.

And he had us.

'Mr Otterwell. Hello. Good to meet you again.' Lenny Spigott came striding down the long, narrow lawn, ducking underneath a line of washing. He was wearing a pair of corduroy trousers and a plain grey shirt with billowing sleeves. There were splashes of colour on both. I thought at first it was pigeon poo. But then I remembered Mr Spigott did paintings – portraits of pigeons: that was his job.

He swapped a handshake with Dad, then, 'Darryl,' he said, turning warmly to me.

'Hello, Mr Spigott.' We shook hands too.

'How's that hen?' He meant Cherokee, of course.

'She's OK,' I muttered.

'I hear she paired up with Duckins' best cock.'

'Mmm.'

Dad frowned and gave me a 'try to make an effort, will you?' sort of look.

I tried, but it was all so easy for him. He didn't have his deadliest enemy lurking behind him, sneering at his back. Why had he *brought* me here? My stomach was churning, my knees felt weak, my head throbbing with Warren's threat: *it isn't over*. He must have been crowing like mad inside.

As if Mr Spigott could read my thoughts he lifted his gaze and said to Warren, 'What are *you* hanging round for?'

'Don't often have visitors, do we?' said Warren. He prodded my shoulder. I leaned away as if a wasp had buzzed me. 'You got squeakers, then?'

'Two,' said Dad.

'Aye, well you would have,' Warren said, smirking. 'One from each egg. That's the usual form.'

'Don't act cocky,' his father warned him.

Warren faked a yawn.

'Come and take a look at my loft,' said Mr Spigott. He put a hand on my shoulder and drew me away. We followed a string of stepping stones up the garden. Pigeon voices began to close in. The flap of wings. The scrabble of feet on hard wooden surfaces. We stepped through a gap in a high privet hedge, and there, spread across the entire lawn, was the biggest pigeon loft I'd ever seen.

It was actually two lofts, side by side, one nearly three times longer than the other. The larger had three sets of sliding doors, with doweled windows to either side. Both were raised a few inches off the ground on what looked like a set of old railway sleepers. They'd been painted brown to blend in with the surroundings. They put my simple shed to shame.

'Very impressive,' said Dad. 'I've stayed in holiday chalets less spacious than this.'

'Forty pigeons want a fair bit of room,' said Lenny. 'Nice aspect for them, too.' He nodded at the shallow fields of crops which stretched out beyond the border of his garden. 'I paint up here, sometimes.'

Dad nodded and looked again at the lofts. 'Is there any reason they're set at an angle?'

Lenny stretched out a hand as if miming a signpost. His shirt sleeve rode up his forearm a little, uncovering a small tattoo: a woman's name – EMILY. The 'i' was dotted with a dripping red heart. I had to tilt my head a little to read it. Warren caught the movement and his gaze narrowed sharply. There was ice in his glare. I quickly looked away.

Lenny said, 'They're positioned south-west to catch the best of the sun, and because of the way I fly my birds. A lot of things govern the way a bird approaches before it drops – wind direction mostly. Happens as well that the sky is clear out there, on the approach. Had it been *that* way,' he pointed to a tall church spire, 'St Barnabas of Barrowmoor might have snatched half my race results. A few seconds' diversion round that spire can make all the difference at the end of a race. I chose this house above five others, purely for the pitch for the birds.'

'Aye,' said Warren, jangling coins. 'Always puts the birds first, don't you, Dad?'

The words seemed to stab Mr Spigott in the chest. I got the feeling there was some sort of feud between them, but Lenny wouldn't rise to it, other than to say, 'Have you done showing off?'

Warren's answer was to press one finger to his nostril and shoot a gob of snot straight onto the lawn. 'I'm going,' he growled. 'Don't wait up.' He glared at me again, then swept away.

With a sigh of despair, Lenny slid back a door on the larger loft. 'Apologies for that,' he said. 'Bit of a handful at the best of times. Anyway, forget about Warren; he's not the reason you're here.'

'Why *are* we here?' I whispered to Dad.

'You'll see,' he said, and ushered me forward.

I joined Mr Spigott on the single corridor that ran the entire length of the loft. 'This one's got three sections,' he said. 'Two for widowhood; one for young birds. The hens and stock birds are in the small loft.'

'Why do you split them up?' I asked.

At the same time Dad asked, 'Widowhood, what's that?'

'Popular racing system,' said Lenny, leading us down to the end of the corridor. He clicked open a lightly-meshed door and led us into an airy compartment. Facing us now were eight rectangular nesting boxes, fixed to the wall in two rows of four. They were slightly different to the one that Greg and Cherokee shared. Instead of a single wooden cage front, each box was split into two distinct halves. The left side looked like a prison cell. It was made from two plastic-coated grilles, fixed at right angles to each other. There was a sliding door in the central grille to allow the birds access (or not) to the 'cell'. The right hand side of the boxes were open. In every space stood a bright-eyed pigeon.

'These are my best old birds,' said Lenny. 'All eagerly awaiting sight of their hens. When you race widowhood, the cocks and hens are kept well apart for most of the week. On Friday nights, I shut the hens up in this side of the box,' he pointed to one of the cells, 'and let the cocks have sight of them for five or ten minutes – only sight, mind, they're not allowed to mingle. Then I basket up the cocks and send them racing.'

'Why?' I said, a bit confused. Greg and Cherokee 'mingled' all the time. I saw Dad smile as if he'd guessed the answer.

Lenny leaned sideways slightly and said, 'When the cock sees his hen he gets a bit excited. He knows that when he returns from his race, his hen will be there and that I'm going to open that little door and let him join up with her for a bit. That's his reward for coming straight home. You'd be amazed how quickly a bird will fly when he knows he's every prospect of mating.'

Dad cracked with laughter. 'And the choosing of the hen, is that important?'

'Oh, aye,' said Lenny, with a gentle wink. 'Fact of life for all us gents, pairing up with the right hen.' He caught my eye and nodded at the birds. 'So, what do you think of them?'

Dad nudged my shoulder. 'Beautiful, aren't they?' He kept his voice respectfully low.

Lenny thudded across the chipboard floor. 'No need to whisper. These old lads are as tame as they come.' He picked a sleek grey bird off the top right box. It had a splash of greeny-purple round its neck and two blue bars across its wings. 'This is Barney Knowall. He was best Channel bird last year. Want to hold him, lad?'

I shook my head. It was like being offered an antique vase. If I didn't hold it right, or I squeezed too hard . . .

'This one fathered your hen,' said Lenny.

My mouth fell open. 'He's Cherokee's dad?'

Lenny nodded, arching an eyebrow. 'Best bloodline I ever had.'

Dad nudged me again. 'That makes him a grandad to Pawnee and Sioux. Potential champions, perhaps, Mr Spigott?'

'Maybe,' said Lenny, putting Barney back.

'On that note,' said Dad, tapping his foot, 'why don't we look at the young bird section?'

My heart skipped a beat. There was something in the way he'd said 'young bird section' that made me feel distinctly uneasy. The words had a coded ring to them. I suddenly had the feeling I was about to find out precisely what we were doing here.

'Youngsters are out at the moment,' said Lenny. 'Let's go and chat in the garden, eh?' He led us out of the widowhood compartment and onto the well-kept lawn again. As I emerged he turned to me and said, 'So, lad. What do you think of the set-up?'

'Brilliant,' I muttered, still unsure of what was happening.

He smiled and seemed genuinely pleased. 'Thing is, forty pigeons is a lot to manage, what with the painting on top. I could use a bit of assistance now and then – a Saturday morning or two for instance.'

So *that* was Dad's plan. A Saturday job. Here? At *Warren's*? My body tightened up like a well-squeezed sponge.

Lenny, unaware of the jolt he'd delivered, calmly took a cigarette out of a packet. 'Couldn't pay you, mind – except in kind.'

I turned to Dad. 'What does that mean?'

He thought for a moment, then he looked me in the eye. 'If you owned a horse – a racehorse, say – one produced from champion stock, you'd want it well looked after, wouldn't you? You'd want it properly housed and fed. You'd want it handled by a real trainer. Someone who knew the sport back to front, who could give it every chance of winning races.'

'Pawnee,' I breathed, cottoning on.

Dad nodded. 'And the other one, the hen.'

'You want me to bring my squeakers *here*?' I turned to Lenny, wide-eyed with fear.

He lit his cigarette and blew a wisp of smoke. 'That's about the rub of it, aye.'

CHAPTER ELEVEN

'Warren's?!' Garry squawked, slipping on a piece of treacherous mud and grabbing at the mesh of the netball courts. 'Why were you going there?'

I bounced back against the mesh, playing with the flaps of my untucked shirt. 'Dad did a secret deal with Lenny. If I work in Lenny's loft on Saturday mornings, he's gonna keep Pawnee and Sioux and train them like proper racing pigeons. If I don't, Dad says I've got to let them go.'

'Flipping heck,' breathed Gazza, flopping back beside me. 'This is major. What you gonna do?'

''Bout what?' said a voice. 'Are you talking about Warren?'

'Aw, no,' moaned Gazza, as 'angel' footsteps sounded behind us. Gemma, Fern and a nervous-looking Suzie were all inside the netball court.

I hadn't spoken a word to Suzie since she'd split on me in Preston's class. And I wasn't in the mood to start again now. She was holding back anyway, picking at her fingers, standing kind of cutely with her weight on one hip. Like the others, she was dressed in her netball kit. A yellow bib with the letters GD was billowing around her sloping shoulders. Her long dark hair, tied in a pony tail, was sitting up high on the back of her head. She rubbed her arms and shuddered a little.

Gemma saw me eyeing her and had to say, 'Got nice legs – hasn't she, Darryl?'

I looked at an interesting clump of mud.

'They'd be all right as lollipop sticks,' sniped Gazza.

'Cheek,' said Fern. 'Suze is a babe.'

'She's a rat,' said Garry.

'You leave her be.' Gemma punched the fence with the heel of her palm. 'She's not feeling very well. You OK, Suze?'

Suzie shivered and looked away.

'What's Warren done to you?' Fern chipped in.

'Spill,' said Gemma. 'We've gotta do netty practice in a minute.'

I sighed and closed my eyes. This lot were worse than Natalie – at her worst. I knew if I didn't clue them in I'd get pestered and plagued for the rest of the week. So I told them about Dad's plan.

'Scary,' said Gemma. 'You gonna do it?'

I told them I didn't have much choice. I couldn't bear the thought of my baby pigeons hobbling about on the street, looking for scraps. No-one was ever going to call them 'vermin'. 'Lenny's coming round on Saturday morning. He's going to put proper rings on the birds so I can register them with the Royal Pigeon Racing Association.'

This didn't draw much sympathy from Fern. 'Wouldn't keep *my* pets near Warren,' she said.

'Yeah,' said Gazza. 'He could poison them or something.'

'Wring their necks.'

'Break their wings.'

'*Shut up!* Just shut up, OK?' Now it was my turn to whack the mesh. Things were bad enough as it was without me having to hear all this.

Then a quiet voice said, 'I think it's good.'

We all looked at Suzie.

'Warren's dad sounds OK to me.' She shuddered. Her teeth chattered loudly. 'Darryl'll get to learn loads of stuff. And Warren wouldn't dare touch a registered pigeon. I think there's a law against it.'

She had a point, but I was so fired up I just exploded. 'When I want your advice I'll ask for it, rat-face!'

'Yeah, like get back on your exercise wheel,' Garry added.

Suzie turned away, her fists to her eyes.

'You rotten pigs,' snapped Gemma, going to her. 'She was only trying to help.'

On the far side of the court another gaggle of players appeared. Miss Coffee, their teacher, was right behind them. She sounded sweet enough but her tongue was like a whip. One crack could make you jump through hoops.

'Time to go,' hissed Garry.

Gemma looked up and sneered. 'That's right, slope off. You don't deserve us, Darryl Otterwell. If Warren Spigott turns you to mince, don't blame us, OK? You didn't have to make Suzie cry. Just 'cos we found out you fancy her, really.'

'He doesn't!' Suzie stamped her foot.

'Fancy her?' said Garry turning back.

'Look at his workbook – the old one,' said Gemma, blowing a wayward curl off her brow. 'He wrote her name and drew *hearts* around it.'

And suddenly, everything clicked. So *that* was why they'd been tagging after us. They thought the SUSAN I'd written on my workbook was supposed to be Suzie McAllister, and that I'd named Suzie Sioux after *her*. Protecting us from Warren was just an excuse; they wanted to get me off with the rat.

Fat chance.

Gazza, though, wouldn't let it drop. As we cut across the school drive heading for the bus, he piped up, '*Did* you write her name?'

I gritted and told him it was Susan Duckins – just a reminder to ring her, that's all.

'Why'd you put hearts around it, then?'

We were close to the bus stop now. A single-decker was ticking over, smoke *phut-phutting* from a black exhaust. We fished out our passes and joined the queue. 'They weren't hearts,' I said hotly. 'They were . . . pigeon prints.'

Gazza wrinkled his nose. He played with the fingers of his hand for a moment, trying to turn them into pigeon toes. 'Pigeon prints wouldn't be heart-shaped,' he figured. 'They'd be like a Y – with a long bit in the middle.'

'Gazza, hearts *are* like a letter Y.'

'No, they're not.'

'Yes, they are.'

'Hearts're too fat.'

'Gazza, shut up.'

'What?'

'Just gag it.'

He looked at me as if I'd just smacked him in the teeth. 'What's buzzing you?'

'Nothing, OK?'

But Gazza wasn't as dumb as he looked. 'You're soft on her, aren't you? Susan *Duck Egg*?'

And now I *was* ready to smack him in the mouth. All that saved him from a trip to the dentist's was a blunt voice saying, 'Only one.'

We ceased swapping scowls and looked into the bus. The driver glanced at us tiredly. 'Toss a coin, lads. Don't have room for you both.'

Garry told him we'd wait for the next one.

'No we won't,' I said, and stepped on fast.

Garry blinked as if he must be dreaming. 'But . . . I'm s'posed to be coming for tea.'

'Looks like tea's off,' the driver said. He whacked a button and the doors swished to.

The bus pulled away up the tree-lined road, leaving Garry like a fallen leaf on the pavement.

CHAPTER TWELVE

I got it in the neck from Mum that night. When I walked in, she asked, 'Well, where is he?'

I was that far out of it I just snapped, 'Who?'

'Garry, of course. The gannet. Your shadow.' She took a peek through the kitchen window as if he might be weeing up the garage wall or something.

'He's not coming.' I slammed my bag onto a stool.

Mum's face played a little juke box of frowns and quickly selected 'Seriously Annoyed'. 'I've got food in the oven for him.'

'He couldn't come, OK?'

'No, Darryl, it is *not* OK!' She threw a tea-towel onto the drainer. 'This is Planet Mum you're on. I am Supreme Being here, remember? You don't dismiss me on a casual whim. I've got a lot on my plate right now and I can do without you on your high horse, thank you. What's the matter with you, anyway? You've been moping around like a wet weekend ever since—'

'Look, just leave me alone, OK?!' And I was gone, up the garden, to be with my birds. As far away as possible from bullies and parents and 'mates' – and girls!

Muttering, I yanked the shed door open. *Whoosh!* Cherokee fluttered straight out. She settled on the bathroom pipe a moment, then blasted off for a spin around the sky. I was watching her circle when Greg appeared at the front of the nest box. He fluttered down onto the floor of the shed, pecked at a couple of grains of corn, ignored them and flapped out onto the lawn.

I went to investigate Pawnee and Sioux.

Barring the occasional glimpse, I hadn't seen the youngsters since they'd hatched. In the afternoons, when I came home from school, Greg was usually glued to the nest. He wouldn't jump off, even if I went round the box with a scraper. Once, when I'd tried to clean around his tail, he'd wooed and buffeted my hand with a wing. So I'd always let him be.

Tonight, for some reason, he'd abandoned his young.

I looked anxiously into the box. The squabs stirred as my warm breath fell upon them. They'd grown quite a bit in the last few days. When they'd first cracked out of their eggs they'd been nothing but helpless bags of skin, hardly able to raise their beaks. Now they looked like swollen prunes, all gawky and goggle-eyed with beaks that seemed too big for their faces. Their feet were splayed out like disused oars. They didn't seem able to stand on them yet.

'Are you OK?' I whispered, pushing my finger towards the nest. The smaller chick – the one I called Sioux – shuddered and nuzzled her brother's neck. Pawnee tipped his beak at my finger. It opened and closed with a gentle *clack*. Then, to my horror, his head fell forward as if all the stuffing had gone from his neck. Sioux blinked and dropped a wing. 'No,' I whispered and hurtled for the phone.

Several times in science, Mr Preston had told us that Nature was harsh and only the fittest of a species survived. What if Greg had left the nest because his hatchlings were ill and he'd given up any hope of rearing them? There were only two people who could answer for sure.

The first of them wasn't at home.

'It's Darryl,' I breathed into Lenny Spigott's

answerphone. 'Please call. It's urgent. It's about the birds. I think Sioux and Pawnee might be sick.'

'What's the matter?' asked Dad, coming past, overhearing.

'Don't know. I've got to ring Susan.' I reached her right away and told her what had happened.

'So?' she said, in a tone that made me feel about two feet tall. 'The babies always look feeble at first. Greg'll be eating green stuff and soil. They do if you let them go natural like yours.'

'But they're leaving food. There was maize on the floor. You don't think they're *all* sick, do you?'

'Darryl, don't you know *anything*? The parents feed the babies on milk for a bit.'

'Milk?' I queried, doodling an S on the telephone pad.

'I don't mean cow's milk, stupid. They make *pigeon* milk from the lining of their crops. It's full of protein and stuff.'

'Oh,' I muttered.

'They'll be all right. Just watch out for cats. They can sniff a nest from miles off.'

'Really?'

'Yes, really. Is that it, now?'

I let the curl of the S develop a whirl. 'You

know tons about pigeons, don't you?'

'Should do,' she muttered. 'I've been helping Grandad since I was eight.'

'Do you miss them – now he doesn't have them any more?'

'A bit,' she sighed. 'Have we finished now? I've got masses of homework to do.'

'No, wait! You know you said about ringing the squabs?'

'Darryl, you have to join a club. And Grandad's really poorly just—'

'It's OK,' I cut in. 'Someone else is gonna do it. A man called Lenny Spigott. He's a pigeon fancier from Barrowmoor.'

There was a pause – a very long pause. Time enough to sketch a heart around the S. 'Lenny Spigott?' Her voice became deeply inquisitive. 'Is he Warren Spigott's dad?'

For a second, all I could do was blink. 'Yes,' I said.

'Do you know Warren, then?'

'He goes to my school,' I heard myself mutter. 'Why do you want to know?'

'Nothing special,' she sniffed. But she sounded different. Slightly guarded. Cagey, almost. 'Just heard the name, that's all. I think a mate of Flick's sister used to go out with him. Flick's my best friend. How'd you wang it, then, about going to Lenny Spigott's?'

So I told her about the journey to Barrowmoor. 'I have to take the birds when they're three weeks old, learn how to train them, then they're going to race.'

'Lucky you,' she said, with a click of her tongue.

I felt bad then, wondering if she might be hurt. She'd only just admitted that she missed being with her grandad's pigeons, and here was me crowing about racing mine.

And then I had a daring idea. 'Do you wanna come?'

The line went silent a moment. 'To Lenny Spigott's?'

'I'd have to ask him properly. But it's bound to be cool, 'cos he knows your grandad. Lenny likes anyone who really loves pigeons.'

She clicked her tongue. 'Dunno,' she said slowly. 'I'll think about it.' Then, in a breath, she was back to normal. 'Gotta go. Or Franky'll be hopping.'

'Who?'

She sighed as if she'd never get away. 'Mr Franke – my history teacher. I've got this stupid project to do. It's on "the indigenous peoples of the North". I have to study the "habitats and

lifestyles of a tribe of Native American Indians".
Two weeks in a tepee. Very cool – not.'

'You have to live in a tepee?'

'Darryl, don't talk thick.'

I winced and was glad there was a phone line
between us. I was glancing in the mirror to check
I hadn't morphed into Garry or something, when
her voice grew inquisitive again and she said,
'Your birds have got Indian names, haven't
they?'

'Cherokee, Pawnee and Sioux,' I said.

'Do you know about them, then? Indians, I
mean?'

I wrapped the phone wire round my fingers.
I hardly knew anything at all about Indians. I
didn't think she'd be too impressed if I told her
they used to fight cowboys a lot. But I could see
where she was going and a germ of an idea was
forming in my head. Before I knew it I heard
myself mutter, 'I know some things about the
Pawnee.'

'Star. You gonna spill for me, then?'

'*Darryl, come on!*' Mum shouted from the
kitchen.

'Can't,' I told Susan, 'my tea's nearly ready.'

'I didn't mean now, this instant, you goop.'

'Oh, yeah. Sorry.'

'It's all right,' she said. 'Forget it. Doesn't matter.'

'No,' I clung on. 'I could tell you, honestly.'

A little breath of air came down the wire. 'Don't bust any brain cells. It's only a project.'

But my brain cells were popping like fireworks now. I was plotting faster than Gran could knit. 'I could write some things down and you could have it . . . on Saturday?'

'Saturday?'

'That's when Lenny's coming round, to ring the birds.'

There was another long pause. 'I'll call you,' she sniffed. 'Better stand back. This phone will explode in one second precisely.'

'Pardon?'

Her receiver went down with a bang.

I lowered mine at arm's length (just in case). But the only thing in danger of exploding was my heart, walloping against my ribs. Me and Susan at Lenny's loft. Yes, it was like a dream come true. Stuff Warren Spigott. He wouldn't dare do anything with Susan around. I beamed into the mirror. A nervous but excited-looking Darryl beamed back. *Pawnee Indians*, I reminded myself. *Gotta work fast. We need top marks info.*

Gold star stuff. My reflection frowned as if to say, 'Great – but how are we gonna get it?' Ha, that was the easy part. *I* might not know about Native Americans.

But Suzie McAllister did.

CHAPTER THIRTEEN

I got up half an hour early next morning and practised my apology in front of my mirror.

Look, I didn't mean to make you yowl. If you hadn't split on me, I wouldn't have bagged off. At least you didn't tell Preston it was Warren. That makes you OK, I s'pose. (Let her fiddle with her hair, then go for the kill.) *Do you want this bag of crisps? Cheese and onion make me vom.* (C&O were her favourites; she ate them all the time. She'd be well impressed. Then we'd walk along and I'd hit her with the rest.) *Did I tell you I'm dead interested in Pawnee Indians?* (Wait for her gob-smacked gob to close, then . . .) *Your dad couldn't lend me a book on them, could he?*

'You're looking rather chipper,' Dad said at breakfast.

'I'm OK,' I said, spooning through my soggies.

He tucked his tie into his waistband and sank into a chair. 'So, did you sort out what was wrong?'

I fired him a blank.

'The birds. Weren't you ringing madam for advice last night?'

'Her name's Susan,' I said. 'She says they're all right.'

He took some toast from the rack and scraped it with butter. 'How's she going to know over a telephone line?'

Mum breezed in before I could snap. 'Tim, hurry up. I don't want to be late.' She dug a golden-coloured aerosol out of her bag and swept into the hall again, fuelled by a burst of sharp-smelling hairspray. I watched her pose by the long hall mirror. She was dressed in a blouse and pleated skirt, not the sweatshirt and jeans she normally wore to take Natalie to school.

'Where's Mum going?'

Dad swirled a cup of coffee. The sickly-sweet aroma drove the hairspray from the kitchen. 'Hospital.'

I stared at him hard.

'A check-up. Nothing to worry about.'

In the hall Mum sighed. 'Oh Natty, not that one.'

Natalie stamped to a halt on the stairs. She tugged at her jumper, turned and stomped noisily back to her room. Mum shouted up to Gran: 'Mum, the green sweater with the bear on the front.' She tutted and raked her hair with a brush.

I caught Dad's eye. 'Is the baby all right?'

He got to his feet, slipped his jacket off the chair and wrapped it round his shoulders with a bullfighter's flourish. 'Go to school. The baby's fine. Your lunch is on the table.'

I leaned over and flipped the box open. Sandwiches, fruit, and cheese and onion crisps.

Well done, Mum.

Spot on.

I looked out for Suzie all the way to school. I often saw her from the back of the bus. She was tall and leggy, easy to spot. She had a fluffy white jacket and a *Mr Man* bag. Gazza always said she looked like an ostrich.

For once, I couldn't see her anywhere. I checked the cloakrooms, the lockers, the computer area, the room where we gathered for registration. Nothing. Then, remembering what a bookworm she was, I went to the library – and found Gemma Thomson instead. She scowled when she saw me coming.

'Where's the ostrich?' I asked.

'I've got this for you, Snotterwell.' She slapped a sealed yellow envelope into my hand. My name was written out neatly on the front.

'What is it?'

'What's it look like, stupid?' She moved closer to cover the note from view. Mrs Renfrew, the upper-school librarian, eyed us as she tidied the magazine rack.

Gemma bundled me behind a bookshelf. '*I* don't think you're worth it. *I'd* have stuck worms in your bag, *I* would. I think you're a miserable *toad.*'

'What are you gabbing about, Thomson? Who's it from?' I held the envelope up to the light. Vommy yellow colour? Nice neat writing? It had to be some sort of drippy—

'It's not a love letter,' she growled. 'Don't rip it, OK?'

I ripped it open regardless. Inside was a single sheet of paper. Primrose-yellow to match the envelope. Gemma bit her lip as I drew it out and read:

Dear Darryl,
  I just wanted to say sorry for splitting on you in science. I did it 'cos my dad has always taught me that bullying is wrong. I was only trying to

*help you, honestly I was. But I shouldn't have
bagged off and made you mad. You don't have to
be my friend, but I hope you will forgive me.*

Yours sincerely, Suzie McAllister

*PS. Gemma and Fern did not make me write
this.*

I couldn't believe it. I had to read it twice to be
sure. Suzie had actually apologized to *me*.

'Well?' snapped Gemma. 'What shall I tell her?'

I shrugged and tried to look . . . moved.

Gemma picked at her teeth and gaped at me
nervously. 'Do you wanna go out with her?' she
asked.

I played it super cool. I told Gemma not to be
dumb. I said 'going out' was a girly thing and
that all you ever did was sit about on walls
sucking lollipops and stuff or walk around at
break with your arms linked up.

She reeled at that and went a bit red. I knew
I'd got her, then. My mind began to plot as fast
as I could think. I reminded her that Suzie had
ratted on me and that no-one could deny it 'cos
everyone had heard it.

'She did say sorry,' Gemma blurted loudly, as
if she was defending every girl in the universe.
Then she went onto the attack herself. 'You like

her, though, don't you? You're whingeing on loads but you haven't said *no*. You wrote her name on your workbook, didn't you?'

'I'm not going out with her, OK?'

'Aw, come on, Darryl. She's ever so nice.'

I played push-pull with a book on a shelf. 'If she's *really* sorry, she's gonna have to prove it.'

'She wrote you a letter! That's major, is that!'

Yeah. The rat liked writing things. She got A* for all her English assignments. Maybe I didn't need a book after all. Maybe . . . I narrowed my gaze and looked Gemma in the eye. 'A letter's no good. I want to know some things about Indians.'

Gemma's nose screwed up like a mis-shapen carrot.

I slung my bag across my shoulder and turned away.

'Wait!' She grabbed my arm and tugged me back. Mrs Renfrew lifted a vigilant eyebrow. Gemma grabbed a book and pretended she was showing me something. 'Whaddya mean, *Indians*?'

'Suzie's dad knows all about them. I want to learn about . . . the Pawnee tribe.'

'What for?'

'I'm interested, stupid . . . 'cos of the pigeons.'

'Oh yeah, them.' She rolled her eyes. When it

91

came to desirable features in the 'going out' stakes, pigeons didn't figure too highly, it seemed.

'Tell her if she writes some good things down – on two sides of paper – I'll be mates with her.'

Gemma's mouth fell open as wide as a bucket. 'Two sides? Just for mates? I'd want a snog every break for that!'

'I'm going,' I sniffed.

She hauled me back. 'OK, I'll tell her. But you'll have to wait.'

Wait? That threw me a bit. Everything had gone really brilliantly till then. I couldn't afford to wait. Not if Susan was coming round at the weekend. I looked at Gemma again.

She saw the panic in my eyes and had a real go. 'Darryl, she's *ill*! Why do you think she's not in school?'

I shook my head.

'She's covered in spots.'

'SPOTS?!'

Mrs Renfrew warned us to be quiet.

Gemma flapped her elbows and (quietly) clucked.

Every bone in my body dissolved to jelly. 'Suzie's got chickenpox?'

Gemma nodded slowly. 'Off two weeks.'

CHAPTER FOURTEEN

'At last! And where have you been?' Mum nodded at the kitchen clock. Quarter past five.

Tch. I wasn't *that* late.

'We were going to send a search party out,' said Gran. Unlike Mum, she had a smile on her face. She seemed to be cooking tea tonight. Something fishy, by the smell of it.

'I've been to the library in town,' I tutted, pulling two textbooks out of my bag.

Dad strolled in as I plonked them on the table. *'The History of the North American Peoples*?' he muttered. 'Bit academic for you, this, isn't it?'

'I'm doing a project on Indians.'

'Well, next time you're doing a "project",' said Mum, 'do you think you could inform me exactly where you are?'

'Oh, Mum! You moan if I don't do stuff – and

now you moan if I do!' I turned to the window. 'I'm going to see—' I stopped mid-sentence. 'Who opened the shed?' My bag hit the floor with a loud thud.

Mum jumped back as if a gun had gone off. 'Me,' she said, holding her tummy. 'You were late, so I let the birds out.'

'Oh, Mum! A cat might get the squabs!'

'Darryl, come back here!' Dad's voice thundered.

Not until I knew my birds were safe.

I hurtled up the garden, all the while looking for Cherokee and Greg. I spotted them high on the roof of the house. Greg was strutting, fanning his tail, turning circles, showing off.

Dad was turning circles of a different kind. 'Darryl, get back here! Do as you're told!'

But I couldn't. I had to check the nest. Heart thumping, I stepped inside the shed. Pawnee sat up when he saw me coming. I didn't get a really good look at Sioux. But she was there. I could see the tip of her beak, resting against the circle of twigs.

'Darryl!'

I leapt out and pulled the door to. 'They're OK,' I said, praying Dad would cool.

'Good,' he said, then tore right into me. *If you thought half as much about your mother's con-*

dition . . . On and on and on it went, ending with the usual, *After tea, you can get straight up to your room – and you can stay there until you're told otherwise!*

No problem. I was doing that anyway, *Dad*.

I spent two hours combing the library books. One hundred and twenty dreary minutes. Although the books contained pictures of Pawnee Indians and there were lots of different references to them, trying to organize the info was hard. By half past seven all I had on my pad was half a page of scribble and a dozen crossings out. I could hardly give Susan that. I kicked *Bison and Braves* off the foot of the bed and buried my face in my pillow, defeated.

I was still chewing feathers when the doorbell rang. Mum called up sourly, 'Darryl, you've got a visitor.'

Garry, I thought, *come to make up*. I clumped downstairs.

'Take your time, I would,' a grumpy voice muttered.

Susan! Oh, wow!

'What are *you* doing here?' I gasped.

'Freezing,' she said, frowning at Mum (who'd deliberately kept her waiting on the step). She was wearing a pair of tight white jeans and a pink crop top with TROUBLE scrawled across it. She shivered and flicked her hair. 'Can I come in?'

'Darryl's been sent to his room,' said Mum.

I gnashed my teeth and looked at the wall. Talk about total embarrassment.

'I've come from Spenner Hill – on the bus,' grumbled Susan.

'The return stop's right across the road,' said Mum.

'Mum?' I barked, fisting my thigh. 'Susan didn't know I'd been grounded, did she? I didn't invite her. She's come because . . .' That was a point; why *had* she come?

'To see the pigeons,' she said, casually examining the back of one hand.

'The pigeons!' I gasped. 'I haven't put Greg and Cherokee in!'

I looked pleadingly at Mum, but her gaze was on Susan. She had a deeply suspicious glint in her eye. 'Half an hour,' she said. 'Then Susan has to leave.' She pulled the door wide. 'In you come – TROUBLE.'

Susan stepped in and flounced down the hall. 'Swanned in like she owned the place,' Mum said later. 'Even pinched an apple from the bowl in the kitchen!'

I didn't care. I liked the way she walked, with

her arms tightly folded and her hips swinging like a fairground boat. She was just so cool. I liked everything about her.

As we walked to the shed I asked a bit nervously, 'Did you really come just for the pigeons?' I was wondering if the project was on her mind.

She took the question another way entirely. 'Don't get any ideas,' she said, scowling at me from head to toe.

I looked away, embarrassed.

She crunched her apple. 'I saw Grandad in hospital this afternoon. He says Lenny Spigott's a top flyer. He says I should check you're doing things right.'

I couldn't argue with that. 'The hatchlings are growing really fast,' I chirped. 'Come and have a look. Pawnee's dead cool.' I opened the door of the shed.

Before Susan could respond, Greg came winging out of the clouds. Without touching a single piece of wood he fluttered to the nest and immediately started to regurgitate food. I could see Pawnee getting really excited. He was bouncing up and down with his stubby wings flapping, shaking his white-tipped beak in the air.

'Weird, isn't it?' Susan said, chomping. 'The

way they vom food up? *Glug. Glug. Glug.'* She mimicked the sound that Greg was making. 'Imagine, feeding on sick?' She put out her tongue. The tip was covered in apple and saliva. 'Must be dead messy. Worse than snogging.'

I wouldn't know. I'd never snogged anyone. I wondered how many times she had.

She clicked her tongue and rolled her eyes over me. 'Did I tell you I've decided to come?'

It took me a moment to make the connection. 'To Lenny's?'

'Yep. You gonna ask him on Saturday? Can't come then. Gotta be somewhere.' She put the sole of one trainer flat against the shed and beamed at me with her big brown eyes.

The sun shone on my life again.

Cherokee fluttered to the roof of the shed. That slowed my pulse a bit. Cherokee equalled Indians equalled library books. Somehow, I had to give Susan the news that the project research wasn't going too well. But as I opened my mouth to speak, she was opening hers – to choke.

'You OK?' I asked, moving closer.

'Apple . . .' she spluttered. 'Get us a drink. Quick.'

I dashed to the house.

'Where's the fire?' asked Dad, as I crashed into the kitchen.

'Susan's choking.'

'*What?*' he squawked.

'She's all right,' I said, filling a tumbler.

'I'll be the judge of that,' said Dad. He dropped his tea-towel and followed me up the garden.

But when we reached Susan, she wasn't all right. She was standing by the shed door, looking pale.

'Susan, what's the matter?' Dad said a little harshly.

'I found it like this on the nest.' She pushed out her hand. There was a baby bird in it. Its eye was closed, its feet splayed out. The beak lay still against her thumb.

I dropped the tumbler. Glass and water sprayed around my feet. 'Sioux,' I gasped. My eyes filled up.

My baby hen was dead.

CHAPTER FIFTEEN

I cradled her stiff little body in my hands, stroking her beak with the edge of my thumb. Even covered in soft yellow down, she felt so horribly cold. 'I don't understand,' I breathed at Dad. 'She was all right yesterday.'

Dad slid a hand round the back of my neck. 'You'd better call Mr Spigott; make sure the other bird's going to be all right.'

'Looked OK to me,' said Susan. 'That one's probably a runt. Would have made a hopeless racer, I bet. Grandad would have culled it, soon as it was fledged.'

'For goodness' sake,' said Dad. He gripped my shoulder and pulled me towards him, telling me to slow my breathing down. I was gasping, feeling giddy and sick. The world was rushing away from me.

By now, Mum was sweeping up the path. 'I heard a crash. Is everything all right?'

Dad intercepted and spoke to her quietly. I heard her stifled gasp.

'Claire, go in. I'll deal with this.'

'I want to see it,' said Mum.

'Claire.'

'I want to see it.'

She appeared at my shoulder. I opened my hands. 'Sioux died,' I said.

'The hen,' she whispered.

'Claire,' said Dad. 'Don't do this, please.'

Mum reached out and stroked Sioux's body. I squeezed my eyes shut. I didn't want to see this. How could I go to Preston's class now and tell them all about pigeon colours? It was then I decided I wanted to bury her. Put her in the ground. Hide the dying away.

'No,' said Dad as I started to babble. 'Mr Spigott should check her. We need to consider the other bird's health.'

'It's bouncing,' said Susan.

But Mum and Dad were in unison now. No amount of argument was going to sway them. Mum said, 'Tim, I think it would be best if you ran Susan home.'

'It's not my fault it croaked,' she said.

'Nobody said it was,' snapped Dad.

'It's my fault,' I wailed, half-stamping a foot. 'I should have checked her properly last night.'

'Sssh,' went Mum. 'It's nobody's fault.'

'Cripes,' went Susan. 'It's only a squab.'

'Come on,' said Dad, and drew her away.

'Bye,' she said tiredly. She flapped a hand and was gone.

Mum look down at Sioux's frail body. 'I'll find her a box. Something safe and warm. We'll bury her as soon as Mr Spigott's seen her. Your dad's right, Darryl: you must ring him.'

'Will you help me?'

She turned me back towards the house. Grandma was waiting on the step. She seemed to know what had happened without having to ask. Mum took Suzie Sioux from my hands. 'Grandma will help you call Mr Spigott.'

'Poor love,' Gran whispered as I flopped into her arms. She kissed my head once and led me to the lounge.

For the second night running, Lenny Spigott wasn't at home. 'It's his answerphone,' I said.

'Leave a message,' said Gran.

I told the machine the story. I cried when I put the telephone down. 'It feels horrible, Gran.'

'I know,' she said, giving me a cuddle. 'Losing a loved one always hurts.'

I thought about Mum, then, and what Dad

had said to her in the garden: *Claire, don't do this.* I knew he'd been talking about the lost babies.

'Gran, can I ask you something?'

'Of course,' she said, stroking my hair.

'What should I have had – more brothers or sisters?'

The collar of Gran's jumper moved with her breath. She ran her hand freely over my arm. 'I'm afraid you'd have been outnumbered, pet.'

'Girls?'

'Hmm. Two lovely hens.'

I sniffed and clutched her hand. 'Will Mum be all right this time?'

'Your mum's a remarkable lady,' she said. 'You mustn't worry about her. Now, how about I make you a nice warm drink and you pop upstairs to bed? You've had a horrible shock. You need to rest.'

'What if I'm asleep and Mr Spigott rings?'

'I'll deal with that. Don't be long going up. I'll bring you some chocolate and a couple of biscuits.' She tousled my hair and left the room.

I sat for a moment in the stillness of the lounge, watching the lava lamp blowing its bubbles. Blue circles crept up the alcove wall and melted mysteriously into the ceiling. I could hear Mum and Gran talking softly in the kitchen, the faraway swish of the wind in the trees, the grinding tick of the mantelpiece clock.

Then the telephone rang.

I picked it up. 'Hello?'

There was silence. A swirl of atmospheric hiss.

'Hello?' I said again. 'Mr Spigott, is that you?'

And then it came.

Woo-oo-oo-oo-oooh! An Indian war whoop.

I jumped in shock and threw the phone down. It break-danced on the telephone table.

Gran's head came round the door. 'Is everything all right, Darryl? Was that Mr Spigott?' She saw the receiver, bouncing on its flex.

'Wrong number,' I spluttered. 'I just dropped it, Gran.' I reached out and put the phone on the hook.

Gran frowned lightly and walked across the room. She picked up the phone and tapped a number. An electronic message squeaked out of the receiver.

You were called today at 20:53 hours.

The caller withheld their number . . .

CHAPTER SIXTEEN

I hardly seemed to sleep at all that night. I lay awake the way I used to when I was a kid, eyes perched on the duvet, knees drawn up, frightened by curtains and wardrobe doors, waiting for something called the bogeyman to pounce. I had always imagined him like a shadow, flitting into corners, rippling over cornices, fingers bent like coathanger hooks, eyes like mirrors, teeth of dust, a voice that creaked like wind-whipped branches. When I was seven, the bogeyman called to me lots of times.

But he never once whooped.

Not until now.

When the doorbell rang and jangled me awake I knew I'd been dreaming – almost dreaming. Floating in the half world between what was real and what was imagined. I heard feet on the stairs and Dad burst in. 'Darryl, up you get. Mr Spigott's here.'

Just hearing the name made me shudder.

'He hasn't got long, so don't hang about.' He grabbed some clothes and threw them on the bed.

'Is it Saturday?' My head was full of sleep.

'No, Friday morning. He's come over specially, because of the bird. How are you? You're looking very peaky.'

I felt like I wanted to wet myself.

By the time I got down, Mum had toast and a hot drink waiting. Gran had taken Natalie into the front. Mr Spigott was chatting to Dad in the garden. He was wearing a flat, peaked cap and a sleeveless grey cardigan. He had a serious look on his thin-boned face.

Mum brought me up to speed. 'Mr Spigott rang after you'd gone to bed. He was very saddened to hear about Sioux.'

I nodded silently and turned to the door.

'Darryl?' Mum said, making me pause. 'What was this other call you had last night?'

I shrugged and told her it was just a wrong number.

'Did they say anything?'

I shook my head.

'Nothing at all?'

I shook my head again.

She turned to the sink looking slightly dissatisfied. 'Take your toast outside. I'll be with you in a minute.'

I joined Dad and Lenny on the patio. 'It's a miserable do,' Lenny was saying, 'losing your first, like this.' He had Sioux in his hands, turning her gently. He saw me coming and widened the arc. 'I'm sorry for you, lad. Really, I am.'

'Thanks,' I muttered, nibbling my toast. It felt so weird, taking sympathy from Warren Spigott's dad.

'Is it possible to know what happened?' asked mine.

'I know what I'd like it not to be,' said Lenny. With an effort, he wrenched Sioux's beak apart. He checked inside her mouth and sighed with relief. 'It's usually canker that gets the young. If she'd had that you'd have seen yellow deposits in the back of her throat, possibly some crusting round the eye, too.' He made me look, then turned her body over. 'First signs of distress in a bird, check the eye, the throat and especially the droppings.' He pointed to her bottom and squeezed the opening gently. 'She's slightly messy around her vent, but not so bad you'd expect any illness. We might learn more from the other squab.'

He placed Sioux's body in a shoe-box Dad was holding and we all trooped down to the shed. Cherokee flew out the moment I opened the door. She whipped past Lenny, who didn't even blink. He strode to the nest box, unclipped the front and put it aside. 'Out you go,' he said to Greg and lifted him away.

Greg wooed loudly and departed for the garden. In the centre of the nest, Pawnee sat up.

Lenny picked him out and examined him carefully. 'Hmm, he looks right enough.' He glanced into the nest box. 'Droppings are normal, perfectly formed. If you see them passing anything green and watery they've almost certainly got a bacterial infection. But that's a healthy nest. And this is a healthy squab, I'd say.' He touched a finger to Pawnee's beak. Pawnee fenced it, looking for food. Lenny nodded and carried him outside. 'He's intelligent, this bird. Just like his mother. Clear, bold eye. He's got racing in his blood.' With that, he dipped a hand into the pocket of his cardigan and pulled out a shining metal ring. Taking Pawnee's right leg in his fingers, he squeezed the three front toes together and slipped the ring over them as far as the pad. Then he bent the fourth toe back and pushed the ring fully onto the leg. He put Pawnee in my hands.

'Congratulations, lad. You now own a certified racing pigeon. GB02Z44488.'

'Thanks,' I whispered.

He put a hand on my shoulder and squeezed lightly. 'I'm only sorry it wasn't two.'

By now, Mum was in the garden and asking if we knew yet what had happened to Sioux.

Lenny tightened his lip. 'Can't say for certain: she may have just been on the frail side.' He took Pawnee and put him in the shoe-box, next to his sister. 'Mind you, look at the difference in size. He's large compared to her. Did the eggs hatch at different times?'

Dad gave me a nudge. 'Yes,' I said. 'Sioux came out the day after Pawnee.'

Lenny nodded in thought. 'That might explain it. The parents don't usually sit the first egg until the second is laid. That way both eggs are incubated for the same amount of time. But occasionally you get an uneven hatching and the first chick develops a slight advantage. If it gets too far ahead the parents can favour it and the weaker one drops. I've fed sick squabs by hand before now, to keep them going till they're able to compete.'

'Are you saying if we'd known that Sioux was in trouble we might have been able to save her?' asked Mum.

'Possibly,' said Lenny.

Dad twisted on his heel and asked me quietly, 'Weren't you anxious about them the other night? You thought they were sick on Wednesday, didn't you?'

'Wednesday? Why didn't you call me?' asked Lenny.

Dad answered for me. 'He left a message on your answerphone – didn't you, Darryl?'

I nodded but couldn't speak. Something was coming. Something bad. The shadow of the bogeyman was in the garden.

Lenny frowned and shook his head. 'That's odd; I didn't get it. I check that answerphone every night. I'll ask Warren when I see him next. Wouldn't be the first time he's taken a message and forgotten to pass the blasted thing on.'

Warren. Suddenly it felt like my head had exploded, sending shock waves through my body.

'Darryl?' said Mum, feeling me quake. 'Darryl, what's the matter? Goodness, Tim, he's shaking like a leaf.'

Dad handed the shoe-box to Lenny and gripped me firmly by the shoulders. 'Darryl?' he said. 'Darryl, what is it?'

'Nnnn . . .' I breathed, trying to say 'No'. 'We could . . . we c-could . . . we c-c-c-c . . .'

'He's having a panic attack,' said Mum.

Dad dropped to one knee and shook me gently. 'Darryl, copy my breathing.'

He counted me through a breathing pattern until I was able to splutter my thoughts. 'We could have saved her . . .' I gasped. 'She didn't have to die . . .'

'All right,' said Dad. 'It's all right now.'

It's not, I thought as the world began to spin. *It's not all right. He killed her. Warren killed her.*

'It happens,' said Lenny. 'No-one's to blame.'

But my head screamed: *No! You're to blame! You made Warren! He's your son!*

'Darryl?' said Dad, through a soup of noise. 'Darryl, what are you doing?'

Darryl . . . Darryl . . . Darryl . . . Darryl . . .

I felt like a spinning top coming to rest.

Mum told me later it was Lenny who caught me.

I'd tried to hit him, she said, as I'd collapsed into his arms.

CHAPTER SEVENTEEN

I didn't go to school that day. Mum said I was 'traumatized' and must have peace and quiet and rest. I spent the whole day doing a jigsaw with Gran.

On Saturday afternoon, Garry called round. Mum let me go to the park with him. We didn't even talk about our falling out. As soon as I explained what had happened with Warren, we were solid mates again.

'Whooped?' he said. He shuddered so much his ice cream nearly wobbled off its cornet.

I lowered myself onto the seat of a swing. 'He was crowing, 'cos his plan had worked. I know he did it on purpose, Gazza. I know he heard the message I left on Wednesday and wiped it off the answerphone so his dad wouldn't hear it. That's as good as killing her, isn't it? Lenny rang last night to say it was OK – the machine, I mean. He said he asked Warren about the message but Warren said he didn't know anything about it.'

'He's a liar.'

'I know.' I twisted, untwisted and twisted again, making the swing chains rattle and clank.

Garry flopped down on the seat beside mine, facing in the opposite direction. 'What you gonna do about Pawnee?' His voice was cautious, purposefully hushed. He was thinking, like I'd been thinking: if Warren had got to Sioux without touching her, what could he do with Pawnee on his doorstep?

'I'm gonna tell Dad I don't want to go to Lenny's.'

'He'll blaze.'

'I know. You gonna help me?'

'S'pose.'

'Thanks.' I stood up and left the swing rocking.

'*Now?*'

'Gazza, come on.'

He sighed and caught up in a matter of strides. We were almost on the edge of the park before he asked: 'Did you bury the other one, then?'

I nodded and told him the story. According to Mum, I'd only flaked out for a few brief moments. They had sat me on the step with my head between my knees. At first, Mum insisted I had to go to bed. But Dad said we ought to bury Sioux first. I heard him whisper, 'How's he going to feel if we wake him up for a funeral service?'

'We buried her near the shed,' I whispered. 'Natalie and Gran came out to watch. I put a feather in her grave and half the shell she was born in. Mum cried when Lenny . . .'

'What?' said Gazza. 'What did he do?'

I squeezed my eyes shut. 'He put a ring on her leg.'

For the next time, he'd said.

Mum cried and cried.

For the next time, Lenny repeated quietly.

Then we'd covered Sioux's body with soil.

I faced Dad in the lounge, with Garry at my shoulder. Mum was sitting on the arm of the sofa. Gran had taken Natalie upstairs for a bath.

'What do you mean, you don't want to do it?'

'Just don't, that's all.'

Mum stroked my wrist. 'Oh, Darryl, why?'

'It doesn't feel right, Mum, now Sioux's dead.'

I exchanged a nervous glance with Garry. We'd discussed this answer all the way home. If Mum didn't buy it, I was really stuck.

She closed her eyes. She'd bought it. So had

Dad; he'd turned away, running a hand through his hair. 'And what are we going to tell Mr Spigott? The man was only round here two minutes ago, registering Pawnee with the pigeon-racing people!'

'Don't know,' I said, with my head in my chest.

Dad turned on Garry. 'Have *you* put him up to this?'

Garry stiffened like a soldier on sentry duty. 'No, Mr Otterwell.'

'Well, try talking some sense into him then. Has he told you what happens if it doesn't go to Barrowmoor?'

Garry stalled.

'We have to let him go,' I said.

'Yes – with a ring on its foot! You do realize people will be finding it for years and continually reporting it missing? I expect the Royal Pigeon Racing Association will get used to it in time. Oh, it's Otterwell's bird, they'll say. The one that could have been a champion racer. The one he was far too lazy to train.'

'It's not like that!'

'It's *exactly* like that.'

'Oh, I can't bear this,' Mum said tiredly. She slapped her hands against her thighs, got up and left the room.

Dad leaned against the fireplace, drumming his fingers. 'I'm *very* disappointed in you, Darryl. I would have thought that the other bird's death would have tightened your resolve, not made you fold before you've even started.'

I turned on my heels and ran into the hall, pausing at the stairwell to clench my fists.

'He's dead upset,' said Garry. 'You don't understand.'

'No, I don't,' said Dad. And he picked up the phone.

He came to speak to me again at tea. He sat at the table, opposite Garry. Mum flicked her fingers over the sink and dried her hands on the corner of her apron.

'I've explained the situation to Mr Spigott,' he said. 'He's disappointed, but says he understands. He suggests you give it another week, see if you feel any differently then. The door is always open, he says.'

'What does that mean?' said Garry.

Dad gave him a look. 'It means that if Darryl should change his mind, the offer is still intact, but because of the nature of the training schedule, Mr Spigott can't take the bird at more than three weeks old. Make a date in your diary, Darryl. And ring it, if you'll excuse the pun.

When the moment comes, that bird goes to Barrowmoor or disappears for good as soon as it can fly. Is that understood?'

I nodded and speared a chip. I didn't need to make dates. My mind was made up. Pawnee Warrior would never go to Barrowmoor.

And nothing would change my mind.

Nothing.

CHAPTER EIGHTEEN

The next two weeks were hard. Getting through school was the worst. I told Gazza not to blab about Sioux to anyone, least of all Gemma Thomson. I couldn't bear the thought of 'Gemma's angels' pestering me about her all the time. I got enough of that in science.

Mr Preston had decided in the very first week that a 'first-hand account of the physical development of *Columba livia* was of great scientific interest' to the class. *Pigeon's Progress*. That's what he called it; a regular update; every Monday, Wednesday and Friday morning.

I talked to the class as if Sioux were alive. I described Pawnee – his strong feather growth, his flappy little wings, his ballooning size (at fourteen days I said he was like 'a coconut marshmallow' and won a shout of 'Splendid!'

from the front), the little press-ups he could do off his still rather clumsy ski-like feet, his squeaking (wow, could he rip) and his first frantic attempts at flight – but all the time I was thinking of Sioux, remembering the soil tipping into the hole, slowly covering her lifeless body. And I felt so mean, so wrong inside, because I was ashamed to admit I'd lost her.

On top of this, there was Warren Spigott.

Eight times I saw him after Sioux's death – kicking round the yard; slouching down a corridor; once, pummelling a boy I didn't know. Six of those times he didn't see me. On the two that he did he stared me out. He never spoke or sneered or gestured or whooped. He didn't even grin. That was the worst. I *wanted* him to grin, to smirk in triumph, because that would have been an admission of guilt. But Warren was clever. He knew about grins. He knew the hurt ran deeper if he kept a straight face. All he ever needed was that ice-cold stare.

If school was bad, Susan Duckins was torture. The day after I told Dad I wouldn't go to Lenny's, she rang, and I had to tell her.

'You're not going?'

'Sorry.'

'Aw, DARRYL!'

My left ear throbbed.

'Why?' she snapped.

I gave her the same excuse I'd given Mum.

'That's useless!' she railed. 'You made me a *promise*!'

I couldn't believe how angry she was. I stood there, filling up, wanting to melt.

'You've ruined *everything*! Do you know that?'

'Sorry.'

Then she huffed and puffed and . . . 'Don't ever build me up like that again!' *Slam!* . . . blew my house down.

I slid down the wall like a lump of slime. I simply didn't think it could get any worse.

Then, one Friday in Preston's class, on the day before Pawnee should have gone to Lenny's, something happened. Something that in time would turn everything around.

The other Susan in my life made a sudden reappearance.

I walked into science and there she was, perched on a desk with her feet on a chair, surrounded by the Thomson gang. I could hear her busily explaining to the others that the chickenpox hadn't been too bad really and that she'd only come back to school on a Friday 'cos she'd missed so many lessons and was mega-bored at home.

'I'd have stayed off, I would,' said Fern. 'Have you got scars from the pox?'

'I've got one *small* scar,' Suzie said proudly. She parted her blouse just above her waist.

'Useless,' said a voice. 'Mine's on my bum!' That was Gazza, pressing in for a sneaky look.

'Gar-ry?!' the girls complained. Then they spotted me.

'Darryl's here!' hissed Fern and they scrambled to their seats. Suzie hastily rebuttoned her blouse.

Gemma tilted her head and chewed on a pencil. 'Hi, Darryl. Suzie's back.'

Suzie smiled at me shyly. She had a slide in her hair with her name printed on it.

'I'm not blind,' I muttered, dropping my bag.

Gemma rolled her eyes between us. Since passing me the note in the library that time she hadn't said a word about the 'mates' deal with Suzie. I'd forgotten all about it. I hadn't even told Gazza. But it was obvious Gemma hadn't forgotten. She cupped her hands around Suzie's ear and frantically whispered something to her. Suzie pulled away, shaking her head. Her hair whipped out like a wet dog trying to dry its fur.

'Go on, do it.'

'*Ge-emm.* Not yet.'

'When?'

'At break.'

Gemma sighed in defeat. I flicked my gaze at Suzie's bag, saw an A4 pad and it all came back. Suzie must have done it – written two sides about the Pawnee Indians. This would mean I'd have to make friends.

At break time.

Pants.

At that moment, Preston walked in. 'Good morning, good morning – and hello, Susan. What a pleasant surprise. Bugs all gone?'

'Yes, sir. Thanks.'

'Good, good, good.' He drubbed the board with a duster. 'I must say it's very committed of you, returning on a Friday. Or could you simply not bear to miss the last exciting episode from Darryl?'

From the desks to my left came a series of snickers.

The front desk creaked as Mr Preston perched his large rump on it. 'Well, come on, Darryl. You know the routine. If I'm not mistaken, today we find out who's won the competition. Are you ready to reveal the colours of your squeakers?'

Garry blew a nervous sigh.

'Pawnee is dark all over,' I gulped. 'His wings

look black from a long way off, but they're really a sort of dark blue pattern.'

'I said that,' someone whispered.

Mr Preston nodded. 'The pattern is known as chequering, everyone. If you looked closely you'd be able to distinguish little triangles of colour all over the wing. Carry on, Darryl.'

'His neck is greeny purple,' I said, 'but his tail and body are greyer than his wings. He's got six white speckles on his head.'

'War paint,' said Connor, ticking his workbook. 'What about the other?'

I saw Garry's fist tighten hard round a pencil. I knew he'd been dreading this. For days he'd been wanting me to tell the truth. He said it was spooky, muttering on about a dead pigeon. It wasn't spooky for me. Sioux flew in my dreams.

To a hushed class I said, 'Her wings are pinky red. She's got one white flight, about halfway along. The rest of her body is white, like a dove.

'Aww,' went several (female) voices.

'She sounds beautiful,' Mr Preston said quietly. 'Thank you, Darryl. You can sit down now.' He slid the board up. 'So, bluey/grey male, red/white female. Put your hand up anyone who had that combination?'

Suzie flapped her workbook.

'This is a swizz,' Fern Summers moaned. 'I've

just got grey. They're always grey in town.'

'You might be surprised to know,' said Mr Preston, 'that there are fundamentally only two types of pigeon colour: ash-red and blue-black. We'll come to greyness in a minute.'

But for the next *forty* minutes he boggled us rigid with a lot of strange blather about chromosomes, genes and some things called gametes – all to prove one thing '. . . therefore, as you can see from the diagram, the ash-red colour is dominant in pigeons to the blue-black colour.'

'So why are they mainly grey?' repeated Fern. She looked around the class for support.

Mr Preston juggled a piece of chalk. 'Although one gene may dominate another, the resulting physical appearance it bestows may not always work to the bird's advantage. Environmental factors play a large part in this. The pigeon is originally descended from the rock dove. Imagine, if you will, a craggy cliff face. On it are perched one thousand rock doves; half are ash-red, leaning to white; the rest are bluey-black, leaning to grey. The rock doves are quietly preening their feathers when a peregrine falcon comes gliding past. He swoops and takes ten birds in all. Eight are red. Two are blue. Why do you think that might be?'

Suzie's hand shot up. 'The falcon can't see the

blue ones so easily, 'cos they blend in with the cliff face, sir.'

'Quite right,' said Mr Preston. 'Their ability to "hide" against their background has given them an advantage over their cousins. In other words, the blue-grey birds are more successful at surviving because they are better adapted to their environment, therefore more of their genes are preserved in the gene pool, therefore the blue-grey colour becomes prevalent. This process is known as "survival of the fittest" and is just one aspect of a much broader term called "natural selection", which we shall discuss in future lessons. Clever use of camouflage is just one of the ways a species might gain an edge over its enemies. Another good tactic is to make yourself so unpalatable that your predator won't eat you.'

'Yuk,' went Gemma.

'Or you might try unnerving your enemy with a fearsome display of colour.'

'Like war paint?' said Connor.

'Like war paint,' Mr Preston said tiredly.

At last, the bell went. 'I want this written up by Monday, please!'

'Sir, what's Suzie's prize?' asked Fern.

'Ah, yes,' Mr Preston hummed. 'A little presumptuous, perhaps, but I thought it might be appropriate, Darryl, if you took Suzie home and showed her the birds.'

'Take her home?' squawked Gazza.

'At their mutual convenience, of course,' Mr Preston said. He smiled and joined the wave of exiting kids.

Gemma seized her chance. 'Do it,' she said and dragged Suzie in front of me.

'Do what?' said Gazza.

'Shut up,' Fern warned him. 'Go on, Suze. Go for it.'

Blushing wildly, Suzie turned to me and said: 'Gem said you wanted to know about Indians.'

'What?' said Gazza.

'Shut *up*,' growled Gemma, curling her lip.

Gazza hissed in my ear. 'What's going on?'

'Later,' I muttered and held out my hand. I just wanted to get this over. All I had to do was take the written sheets, tell Suzie we were quits and go. As for her seeing my birds – no way.

She took a deep breath. 'I asked my dad about the Pawnee tribe. He said there was too much for two sides of paper, unless you were specific about what you wanted.'

'Get to the good bit,' Gemma pressed, anxiously chewing her hair.

'So Dad said he'd be pleased to talk to you about it.'

'Look at him,' Gemma interrupted again, 'and smile – with teeth.'

Suzie took a breath and smiled (with teeth). 'So . . . would you like to come for tea next week?'

'WHAT?!' screeched Gazza. He grabbed my arm and hauled me away. 'You can't,' he whispered. 'You can't do that.'

'Why?' I asked. My brain felt numb.

He twizzled and threw up his hands in horror. 'It'll mean you're *going out* with her, won't it?!'

CHAPTER NINETEEN

Before I could pinch myself to check I wasn't dreaming, Miss Coffee swept in and chased us from the room. 'Get along, you lot. I've a lesson to prepare.'

'Yes, miss – thanks!' Gazza towed me to the door.

'Darryl?' Gemma called. 'What about . . . ?'

But I was gone, legging it down the corridor. Not really knowing why. Just running, running, running – to the one place the girls couldn't reach us: the toilets.

'What's going on with the rat?' asked Gazza. He hotched his bag across his shoulder, unzipped his pants and had a quick pee.

I slapped my face with water and told him the deal: why I'd wanted the Pawnee info.

'You were gonna do the Duck Egg's homework for her?'

I gobbled a drink from the water spout. 'No, stupid, *Suzie* was.'

He sat up on the radiator, heeling the fins. 'Cool. You secretly going with the Duck Egg, then?'

'Gazza, stop calling her that.'

'She's a girl,' he said. 'We always bag them off.'

I snatched a paper towel from one of the dispensers. 'I'm not going out with Susan Duckins. She hates me. She—'

'Sssh!' he went suddenly. He leapt off the rad and gripped my arm.

Warren Spigott's cocky voice echoed down the corridor.

We dived for a cubicle and locked the door. 'Stand on the bog.' Gazza plonked down the seat. 'I'll sit. If they play "sweep" and see four legs, we're dead.'

I scrambled up as the doors crashed open.

'Smells worse than my grandma's pants in here.' The voice belonged to Ginger, Warren's best mate. 'Got a smoke?' he asked as one of them broke wind.

'Set fire to that if you want,' said Warren.

Ginger laughed and said, 'One way of blowing this frigging dump up. Come on, gizza ciggy.'

Urine splattered loudly against the pans.

'Forgot to raid the old man's pack. I'm out.'

'Where's that Otterwell kid when you need him?' sneered Ginger.

Garry winced and tightened a fist.

Ginger said, 'He still coming round to your gaff?'

I heard the sound of a zip. Warren's boots clip-clopped against the hard-tiled floor. 'Nah, big chief Warren sorted that.' He let out a fearsome whoop.

Garry, startled, pressed himself back. I grimaced as his shoulder blade cracked my knee. My right foot slipped off the edge of the seat. As I moved to correct my balance the back of my head clonked against the loo cistern.

'Whassat?' said Ginger.

Garry lifted his feet and pressed his soles against the cubicle door. A fist hammered hard against the other side.

'Oi! Oi! Oi!'

I heard a shuffle of clothing and knew that one of them was crouching down to see.

'Empty,' said Ginger. He banged the door again. 'How come it's locked?'

'Health alert,' said Warren. 'It's probably bunged up with your rancid jobbies.'

'First years' heads, more like,' replied Ginger. 'That's what you should have done with Otterwell: flushed him – and his birds.'

I felt Garry shudder.

'Tell you summat,' said Warren. 'There's been an interesting development on the Otterwell front.'

My shoulders stiffened. Development? What development?

'Yeah? Lend us your comb a sec.'

'Stuff off! Don't want your ginger fuzz in my thatch.'

'Miserable git. What's going down, then?'

Warren's boots scored the tiles again. He was heading for the door, voice fading all the time. 'I was couching it round at Laura's last week—'

'What, rabbit teeth Laura? You still knocking that dog?'

'—she comes in handy, if you know what I mean. Now shut up and listen. This is kinda tasty. I'm there, right, just getting good and friendly, when Laura's kid sister turns up with . . .'

The toilet doors crashed to.

'Aww . . .' went Gazza, sighing with relief.

I scrambled over him and flipped the lock.

'Come on, we've gotta follow them. We've gotta find out what he was going to say.'

'No chance,' spluttered Garry. He sauntered out, adjusting his pants. 'If he sees us tagging him he's gonna go mental.'

'Yeah? Well, he's not the only one, is he?!' I ran to the cubicles and kicked a door hard. It slammed against the wall and flapped back, shuddering. The uppermost hinge had sheared right off.

Sausages, as Natalie would say.

We stood there a moment, digesting the shock.

Then the panic took hold, and we ran.

CHAPTER TWENTY

The rage stayed with me all day long, grinding into me, building fear. The worst fear possible: the unknown terror.

What had turned up at Laura's house?

With her kid sister?

Laura *who*?

I tried endlessly to work it out. It didn't go unnoticed that my mind was 'awol'. All day I was ordered to 'wake up', 'sit up' or 'pay attention'. During history Mr Halliwell asked, 'How were things in fairyland, Darryl?' as I seemed to be away with the 'little sprites' a lot.

Gemma Thomson thought it was love. Luckily, I'd managed to avoid her since science – not that she hadn't tried to bug me, of course. Halfway through IT she caught my eye, pointed at Suzie and rolled her mouse up and down over her heart. Mr Anwar tapped her with a mouse mat and turned her to face her monitor again.

It was geography, last lesson, where it all went wrong.

Mr Pusey set us a map-reading exercise. 'You may do this in pairs,' he said.

'Boring,' said Gazza.

Mr Pusey split us up. 'Garry, take your map to Donna, please.'

Donna Barker clapped a hand across her eyes.

'Darryl, you work with Suzie today.'

For ages, we didn't even look at one another. I read the questions; she worked out the answers. I watched the ends of her dark hair brushing against the map. She traced contours with it, rode railways, crossed streams. She didn't once loop it or try to pin it back. Hiding, I thought. Keeping her distance. That suited me fine. My head was swimming anyway – with Laura and Warren.

'Post Office,' she said. 'Question nine.'

Yet, I couldn't stop thinking about her invite. Despite all the horrible things I'd said, she really was trying to be helpful. Sitting there, watching her concentrate, I began to appreciate how brave she'd been to write her note. And I knew, deep down, it was the wrong way about. It should have been me who was saying sorry. I'd tried to use her, to impress Susan Duckins. I was the rat, not her. In some ways, I owed her so much. She'd been the one to name Pawnee, and guess Sioux's colours, and protect me at the chip shop. She—

'Post Office,' she repeated. 'Darryl, you OK?'

I looked away, afraid I was going to crack.

Now she did loop back her hair. 'It's OK,' she said. 'About tea, I mean. I know you don't want to come really. And if Preston asks me about your birds, I'll make something up. Post Office. Write it down.'

I drilled my pen into the corner of my work-book. 'Can't. Not now.'

Her eyes fastened on the pen. 'Can't what? What do you mean?'

'See them. Can't see my birds.'

'I know,' she said quietly, sounding hurt. 'I just meant—'

And then it came out in a rush: 'Sioux's dead.'

Suzie blinked in surprise. For a moment she gazed at the map as if the answers she was seeking were contained within its whorls. 'But you were talking about her in class this morning, as if—?'

'I made it up.'

She blinked again and reached for a pair of dividers. 'Pukey's watching. Look at the map.'

She nudged my foot. 'What happened to Sioux?'

I shook my head.

'Was it Warren?' There was fear in her soft voice now.

I started to pant.

She touched my hand. 'It *was* him, wasn't it?'

'I've gotta go,' I croaked. 'He might come for Pawnee.' I pushed my chair back and grabbed my bag.

'Darryl, slow down. You're not making sense.' Suzie reached for my arm. I batted her away.

Mr Pusey looked up from his desk. 'Darryl? Susan? What's going on?'

'Darryl's not well, sir. He—'

The bell went. I ran.

'Darryl?' said Mr Pusey. 'I haven't given permission—'

But I didn't need permission. I was out and running. Through school, past the tennis courts, the tree-lined drive. I didn't stop until I hit the front seat of the bus.

'Timed that right,' the driver said.

The doors swished shut and I was on my way home.

Gran was washing pots when I swept in, breathless. 'You're early,' she said. 'What do you fancy for tea?'

I dropped my bag and peered out of the window. The shed looked sound. 'Where's Mum?'

'Upstairs, having a rest. Darryl, what's the matter?'

'Has anyone tried to see the birds, Gran?'

She shook her head, puzzled. 'Are we expecting someone?'

'If anyone comes, you mustn't let them in.'

She patted a stool. 'Darryl, sit down. You're flustered. What is it?'

'Can't, Gran. Not now.' And I was gone. Up the garden, straight to the shed.

Panting heavily, I opened the door.

And there was Pawnee.

Out of the nest box.

Perched on a can of paint on the floor.

With a *whoo* Greg and Cherokee fluttered out. Pawnee squeaked and turned on his can. 'It's all right,' I whispered. 'I've come to protect you.' I stepped forward and gathered him into my hands. The toes of his ringed foot clamped around my thumb. He jabbed his head for a view of the garden. 'Yes, you can go out soon,' I whispered. 'When I set you free you can fly where you like.' A tear teetered on the corner of my eye. It wasn't fair. I didn't *want* to let him go. If it hadn't been for Warren . . . 'You've got to go back in the box now,' I sniffed. But as I turned to the nest he gave a loud, shrill squeak. And very quickly I understood why.

Another egg was lying in the nest.

I settled Pawnee on a corner of the workbench and took the new egg out of the box. It was warm and smooth, sleeping with life. Another pigeon, wrapped up inside it. Another squab for Warren to kill. 'I hate you,' I whispered. 'I hate you. I hate you.'

I put the egg down and yanked the box up, swept to the door on a sudden rush of anger. 'I hate you!' I screamed and kicked the box hard. It tumbled across the lawn like a dice, leaving a trail of feather dust and twigs.

I kicked it again. Greg fled roofwards.

'You'll never get another one!' I shouted at the sky. *Without a nesting box*, my mind was screaming, *there would never be another pigeon to hatch*.

I held the box by the doweled front and banged it on the grass.

'Darryl!' two voices cried in unison.

Someone came hurtling up the path. Not Gran. Not Mum. Someone younger and fitter.

Suzie McAllister grabbed my arm. I pushed her aside and slammed the box again. With a crack, the catches broke and the front came away from the main compartment.

'Darryl, stop it! Or I'll have to make you!'

I lashed at Suzie again.

And suddenly, the sky was rolling. I felt myself tumble over her back and land with a thud, face flat to the lawn. She pressed a foot hard in the centre of my back and held my arm upright, tight and locked.

'Goodness,' gasped Gran. 'Where *did* you learn that?'

'I'm sorry, Mrs Otterwell, I had to stop him.'

'I'm his gran,' said Gran.

'Let him go,' growled a voice from further back. Mum.

Suzie released me. I curled up like a baby.

Mum cradled me into her arms, gentle and furious all in one. 'Just who do you think you are, young lady?'

'I'm Suzie, from school,' Suzie said repentantly.

'Well, Suzie from school, this had better be good. I want to know *now* what this is about!'

Suzie dropped to one knee. 'I'm sorry,' she whispered, touching my arm. She looked once at Gran, then back again at Mum. 'He's being bullied by a boy called Warren Spigott,' she said.

CHAPTER TWENTY-ONE

'Why didn't you tell us it was him?' said Dad. He was pacing the lounge like a caged wolf. Arms folded. Tie loosened. Shirt sleeves rolled. His face showing no emotion whatsoever.

'Tim, please, you'll wear the carpet out,' said Mum. She was sitting in an armchair, fussing with a tissue.

On the sofa beside me, Suzie, sitting very prim and proper, gave me a gentle nudge.

'Dunno,' I mumbled. What *can* you say?

'And what exactly did he do to you?'

I looked sideways at Suzie. She gave a little nod. For the first time ever, I spilled it to my parents. Whatever Warren had commanded, I'd done.

'Oh, Darryl. Why didn't you just say?' said Mum. There was so much sadness in her voice

– as if she felt she'd let me down. 'We would have helped you. We would have understood.'

'I was scared to, Mum.'

'Did he hit you?' asked Dad.

I shook my head. 'Only arm twists and stuff.'

He swept past, tracing his brow with his fingers.

'But didn't that letter from the school put an end to it?' Mum crumpled her tissue, pulled another from the box.

Suzie explained about Warren at the chip shop and how he'd said it wasn't over. And I told them, then, about the answerphone message and how I knew it was Warren because of the whooping.

'That's horrible,' said Suzie, tightening a fist.

'It's disgusting,' Mum added, becoming very angry. She looked wild-eyed at Dad.

At last, he stopped pacing. 'And this is why you changed your mind about the pigeons, because you were worried he'd hurt Pawnee?'

'What?' said Suzie, looking shocked.

I hung my head.

'Oh, this is appalling,' said Mum. 'Something has to be done about this.'

Dad nodded, tight-lipped, and checked his watch. 'Go and tidy the lawn, you two.'

I looked up. Was I in trouble or not?

'Go on,' he said quietly, showing me nothing. 'Your mum and I need to talk.'

Suzie nudged me again and we left the room together.

The door closed quietly behind us.

For a while, it was like it had been in geography. We didn't speak much, just tidied the lawn as Dad had said. I found a screwdriver in the shed and together we set to work repairing the nest box. Suzie held the cage front, applying forward pressure, while I screwed the catches back in place.

I was on the second catch when she said, 'Do you hate me?'

I paused and shook my head. 'I'm sorry I called you a rat.'

Her pale cheeks flushed. 'It's OK,' she said quietly. She looked up and quickly made rat's teeth at me.

I bit back a laugh. 'You won't tell anyone you threw me, will you?'

''Course not,' she said, frowning hard.

I nodded. We finished the catch.

'What do you think your dad will do?'

I shrugged and pushed the cage front back onto the box. The catches were stiff, but they just about worked.

'Perhaps he'll let you keep Pawnee now?'

'No chance.' I shook my head. 'There's another egg, too.'

As if by magic, Greg flew into the shed in search of it. He angled his line of vision towards that place where his box should be. Pawnee fluttered down to his side.

Suzie turned to look. 'That him?' Wings outstretched, Pawnee was chasing Greg round the shed floor, pestering for food and squeaking for England. 'Cor, he doesn't half make a racket.'

I nodded. 'Dad bags on loads about it. He woke up early three times last week. He says the squeaking is upsetting his biological clock.'

Suzie laughed and shook her hair. 'Well, I think he's sweet – like a sort of kitten pigeon. Aah, look at his speckly bits. Aw, Darryl, you *can't* let him go.'

'Got to,' I muttered. 'Or Warren's gonna get him.' The smiles departed. A black cloud settled over me again.

Suzie swung herself into a cross-legged position, adjusting her skirt so it covered her knees. She picked a blade of grass and pulled it through her fingers. 'How? He can't touch Pawnee now. And he just got lucky with Sioux.'

'You don't know Warren. He's really got it in for me.' And I told her then what I'd heard in the toilets, and how desperate I'd been to work out what his girlfriend's sister had 'turned up with'. 'What if it's an air gun – or a falcon or something?'

She gave me a look Susan Duckins would have envied. 'Darryl, people's kid sisters don't carry guns or birds of prey. It's got to be more devious than that. What was the name of Warren's girlfriend again?'

'Laura.'

She nodded and picked at the grass. 'We need to find her second name, then check out her sister.'

'How?'

'Angels have ways,' she said.

Just then, a door banged to in the kitchen. I heard strained voices. Mum and Dad.

'Come on,' whispered Suzie with a finger to her lips. We crept to the kitchen and crouched beneath the window.

'Character-building?' I heard Mum say. 'You can't be serious? Look what the poor soul's been through already. I don't care what guarantees you've got. That's tantamount to cruelty, Tim.'

'Cruelty?' hissed Suzie as Dad said his piece.

'I think it's the right way – and so does Spigott. I'm happy to let him deal with it.'

'They're going to kill him,' I tremored; 'wring Pawnee's neck.'

Suzie frowned and shook her head. 'They wouldn't do that.'

I jumped to my feet and chased towards the shed, just as Dad stepped into the garden.

'Darryl, can you come here, please?'

'You can't kill him!' I shouted, whirling around. 'Leave him alone! All of you!' I grabbed the screwdriver, gripping it tight, ready to defend us both if I had to.

Dad set his jaw straight and stared at me hard. 'No-one is going to kill anything,' he said. 'Now put that down and stop being silly.'

Suzie planted herself at my side. 'Darryl, listen to him. Please?' She pushed her hand into mine, took the screwdriver from me and dropped it on the lawn.

'Thank you,' said Dad. He looked me in the eye. 'I've had a long chat with Mr Spigott. He's appalled by what's happened and will be talking to Warren, and the school. We didn't see eye to eye on everything, but there's one thing we are united about: bullying, in any shape or form, shouldn't be allowed to interfere with what's right and proper for you . . . or the bird.' He looked up the garden. Pawnee had come to the threshold of the shed. He beat his wings like helicopter blades but failed to move a feather-width in any direction. The art of take-off was, as yet, beyond him. But it wouldn't be long coming, and Dad knew it. 'You wanted to fly him: that's what you'll do. Tomorrow morning, I'm driving you to Barrowmoor, Darryl. Pawnee is going to be a racing pigeon.'

CHAPTER TWENTY-TWO

Sometimes I felt that Dad had it in for me almost as much as Warren did. I didn't question his decision. I knew it would be pointless. Once his mind was made up on a matter of 'principle' he wouldn't be shaken. That was his way. But I knew, and Mum knew, and Suzie admitted later after tea, that Warren would never give up the fight. I might just as well have smacked my palms into his chest and challenged him to meet me behind the bike sheds.

It wasn't over.

The drive to Barrowmoor the next day was tense. Dad didn't say much, just a few tired lines about 'privileged opportunities'. It was only when we turned into Station Road that he took a deep breath and mentioned Warren. 'I'm not coming up to the house,' he said. 'You'll be quite safe; I've arranged with Mr Spigott that Warren won't be there.'

I nodded, tight-lipped, and unclipped my seatbelt.

He sighed and pinched the bridge of his nose. 'I haven't abandoned you, Darryl. I'm doing this because I believe it's right and because, more than anything, I believe in you. If you hold your head high, you and the bird will both come out winners.' He paused and ran his hands around the steering wheel. 'Go on. I'll be back, on the dot, at two.'

I walked up the sloping herring-bone drive, carrying Pawnee in a box against my chest. He was squeaking softly, trying to stay balanced. For a moment I thought about letting him go, pretending I'd dropped him, saying the box had fallen open. But in my heart I knew that was a coward's way out. Whatever trials I faced, we faced together. And the first was almost upon us. As I steadied myself, the house door opened . . .

. . . and Mr Duckins stepped out.

'Now then, what have we here?' His voice was gruff, like a great woolly bear. He looked tired, leaner, older in the face. It was easy to see he hadn't been well.

'Hello, Mr Duckins. It's good to see you.' And it was. Really good. In all this madness, Alf was like a friendly dependable giant. I felt safe and confident with him around. I glanced at Lenny. He smiled inwardly, knowing he had a way to go yet before I'd show him the trust I gave Alf.

'New recruit,' said Lenny, nodding at the box. 'The squeaker, out of Gregory Peck.'

Alf lifted a bushy eyebrow. 'Let's see it then, lad.'

I put the box down and released the flaps. Pawnee squealed as I reached in to grab him.

Alf took him in his hands like a loving grandad. 'Aye, not bad. Skinny, but he'll grow.' He smoothed the tail feathers, fanned a wing. 'Do you know what he is, lad? How to describe him?'

'Dark chequer pied,' I said, straight up.

Alf grunted in approval. 'Mmm, good. Glad to see I've taught you something.' He squinted at Pawnee's inquisitive eye. 'Nice eyesign, Len. Very bold. Could be a good 'un this one, you know. Almost makes me wish I were flying again.'

'We're hoping for great things,' Lenny told him.

Alf nodded and handed Pawnee back. 'See you pay attention to what this chap tells you. He's the best there is. Don't play him up.'

'No, Mr Duckins,' I said politely. Crikey, for a

moment he'd sounded like Susan. I could see her faintly, in his eyes.

'Aye,' he murmured, and held me a second with a gaze that was somehow faraway and near. It was as if he wanted to see in me something of the boy he'd once been himself. 'You'll do all right,' he said. He ruffled my hair, flapped a hand and was gone. It felt like the baton had been transferred. Now it was me – and Lenny Spigott.

'Nice surprise for you, seeing Alf,' he said, beckoning me forwards into a room that looked more like an art gallery than a lounge. Pigeon paintings covered the walls. More were stacked in an alcove, by the fire. On the TV I saw two family photos. One of Lenny and a woman at the seaside. One of the woman alone, close-up. Nothing whatsoever of Warren.

'Does Mr Duckins come here a lot?' I asked, as we went through a set of tall French windows, into the sunshine on the garden side. It was a beautiful morning, still and warm. Sparrows twittered round a stone bird table. St Barnabas of Barrowmoor chimed the hour.

Lenny shook his head. 'Known him twenty years, through club and pub, but it's only the second time he's visited the house. Bit odd, really, as if he was paying his last respects – to the sport, I mean. I think he's missing it. He'd be proud to see you do well with that bird.'

I stroked Pawnee with my thumb.

Lenny took a delicate breath. 'Let's get the hard stuff done with, eh? Then we're on an even footing. I've had it out with Warren, about this bullying. He says it's a heap of something and nothing – which is what you'd expect him to say, I suppose. I wanted him to prove it by shaking your hand, but he wouldn't have it. That's his choice. Warren thinks he's a man but he still has a lot of growing up to do. I've warned him he's not to bother you again. He knows you'll be coming here, regular, on Saturdays, but I doubt you'll ever see him. He's usually up the town, chasing some girl. As for the bird . . .'

I looked up nervously.

'. . . Warren doesn't know you're bringing one here, and there's no obvious reason he should. I'll be discreet, entering young 'un in my book. He'll be safe; I give you my word. Now, let's find a home for him, shall we?' He slid open the nearest door of the loft.

'Where are the old birds?' I asked right away. All the widowhood boxes were empty.

Lenny glanced at his watch. 'At a rough guess, over Northamptonshire. They won't be back for a bit. Barney's in a sprint – sharpener for a big prize race next weekend. He should be home in about ten minutes.'

He opened another fine-meshed door and led me into a small, square space where a dozen or more birds were strutting around. A large rack of box perches, like the 'pigeon-holes' outside the staff room at school, took up the whole of one wall. Our entry caused a general kerfuffle of flight. Birds began to circle from the floor to the perches, squabbling over the highest settles.

'Youngsters,' said Lenny. 'They're a comical lot.'

I nodded, shaking a bird off my head.

'Yours needs to spend a week or two in here,' he said. 'Once he's acclimatized, we'll go from there.'

'Will we be able to race him?'

Lenny took Pawnee and settled him into his confident hands. 'He's a long way behind the others, lad. He's what we call a late bred – a very late bred. I'll have to think his schedule through pretty carefully. If he trains up well and I'm happy with him, we might fly him once or twice towards the back end of the season, just to give him a taste of what it's all about. Nothing flash; he won't be ready for the big events.' As if to prove it, he lobbed Pawnee into the flock. With an awkward flurry of wing beats, my squeaker broke his fall and pattered indignantly across the floor to perch himself on an upright house-brick. 'Talking of late breds, what have you done with the second round of eggs?'

I looked at him, surprised. 'How did you—?' I blushed and felt completely stupid. Even standing here, in the middle of his loft, it was easy to forget he was an expert with pigeons. 'They're under a plant pot in our shed.'

'Dad wants them ditched, I s'pose?'

'He doesn't know about them yet.'

Lenny chuckled and stroked his chin. 'If it's OK with you – I'll ring Dad and ask him to bring them when he collects you. I'd like to have a look at those eggs. Might be something I can do – to check if there's a problem with the female line.'

'OK,' I said quietly, though I couldn't imagine how two cold eggs could be of much use. What could he possibly do with them? Weigh them? Look at them under a microscope, perhaps? I was too frightened of showing my ignorance to ask.

Suddenly, he swept his watch arm up. 'Time to keep a look out for Barney. Come on.'

I glanced at Pawnee, standing proudly on his brick, then followed Mr Spigott into the garden.

'Shout if you see him,' he said.

Almost immediately I spotted a bird near St Barnabas' spire. 'Up there.'

Lenny turned to see. 'No, that's a wood pigeon.' He panned the horizon. '*That's* a racing pigeon.' He pointed west of the spire.

In the blue sky above the open fields, a bird was fast approaching. At first glance, it appeared to be travelling at an angle that would take it hopelessly wide of the loft. Then, in an instant, it banked towards the garden, losing height so rapidly it looked in danger of crashing to earth. As it dropped, its flight path levelled, until it was skimming across the fields barely a metre or so off the crops. It was heading straight for the loft.

'It's going to hit the middle doors,' I said.

Lenny calmly took a cigarette out of a packet. 'Best get on and open them, then.'

I realized then that he'd arranged this for me. A first lesson in novice pigeon racing. I sprang to the doors and pushed them back. Ten seconds later, Barney thumped onto a landing board, pottered down the corridor and flew to his box.

'Go fetch him, then.'

'*Me?*'

'Aye. You're the one needing to learn.'

I gulped and dived into the loft. After six attempts, I managed to catch Barney and carry him outside.

Lenny blew a smoke ring into the sky. 'See that sleeve of rubber on his leg?'

'Yes.'

'That's what's known as a race rubber. The number stamped on it matches with a docket that's kept at the club. We need to clock it to record his time.' He rolled the rubber off Barney's leg and popped it into a thimble-shaped object. 'This thimble goes in there.' He pointed to a timing clock, sitting on a stool just inside the loft. Alf Duckins had shown me one of these once. It was about the size of a large metal cash box. In the top of the box was a square-shaped hole. Lenny dropped the thimble into it and struck a lever. The thimble disappeared into the body of the clock.

'That records the time on a paper roll,' he said. 'Tonight I'll take the clock to my club. Our secretary will open it, calculate Barney's velocity, then we'll see how he's fared.'

'Will he win?'

Lenny laughed and shook his head. 'In the time it took you to grab hold of him, lad, Joe Farmilow up the road will have clocked in six.'

'Sorry,' I whispered.

He clapped my shoulder. 'You'll get quicker. Right now, my main concern is what your mum's going to say about that top.'

155

There was a large streak of pigeon poo down my sweatshirt. Cheers, Barney. 'Doesn't matter,' I shrugged. 'When I get home, I've got to get changed and have a shower, anyway.'

'Going out?'

I gave a sheepish nod.

'Relations?'

Uh-uh. Scarier than relations.

Tea at Suzie McAllister's.

CHAPTER TWENTY-THREE

On the doorstep I gave her feathers. One from Cherokee. One from Greg. Her eyes lit up like a couple of stars. She quickly pushed the feathers into her scrunchie, then pulled me inside, crying, 'Mum, look what Darryl's brought me!'

She dragged me into a bright blue kitchen and performed a ballet-dancing, shoe-clattering twirl. She was wearing a pair of flared denim jeans and a top that read: I GOT MY LOOKS FROM MY MUM, MY BRAINS FROM MY DAD, AND THIS T-SHIRT FROM SANTA. Tacky, but she did look cute.

Mrs McAllister, a stouter, shorter-haired, version of her daughter, seemed to be caught between a smile and a scowl. 'Yes, very nice (scowl at feathers). Hello, Darryl (half-smile at me). Are they— (scowl at feathers again)?'

'From his pigeons?' Suzie interpreted. 'Yes.'

Mrs McAllister stood on tiptoe to inspect them. 'They are quite *clean*, I hope?'

'Oh, Mum. Darryl delouses his pigeons – don't you?'

I grimaced.

Mrs McAllister winced.

At that point Mr McAllister walked in. He examined the feathers with a studious squint. 'Now, miss, if you were true Pawnee, these would probably be eagle quills. I deduce they are pigeon and that this young man is therefore Darryl.'

'This is my dad,' Suzie said, linking arms. 'He's bonkers, but he does know loads about Indians.'

Mr McAllister reached across the room. 'Pleased to meet you, Darryl.' He extended his hand, nearly crushing me in his grip. He was dressed in a pair of tracksuit bottoms and a white cotton top that seemed almost shrink-wrapped over his muscles. He had short, dark hair and a thin moustache. When he smiled, his eyes had a cheeky twinkle. Gran would have really fancied him. 'I think tea's a few minutes away yet,' he said, 'so let's go into the lounge and have a powwow, eh?'

He led the way through and pointed me

towards a large yellow sofa. The room was sparse. Clean and modern. Polished wooden floor. Craning lamps. In the alcove beside me was a tall glass cabinet, filled with trophies and medals on plaques. As I leaned in trying to read an inscription, Suzie's dad sat down in an armchair and said, 'Been collecting them since she was eight.'

I glanced at Suzie, perched on a padded footstool opposite. A thick white rug was spread across the floor like an ice floe between us. 'Dad, Darryl's not interested in judo.'

Her father took the opposite view. 'Wouldn't tangle with her if I were you, Darryl. Unless you know her weakness, of course . . . *Very ticklish*,' he mouthed before Suzie could see. 'So, what do you want to know about the Pawnee?'

I shuffled uncomfortably and looked at Suzie. She tickled her chin with my gift of feathers. Something gnawed at me deep inside. It was her I was here for, really, not Indians.

'I think Darryl just wants to know anything, Dad. He's got a bird called Pawnee Warrior. It's being trained as a racing pigeon. It'd be great if Darryl knew what sort of people the Pawnee were, then he might think of his pigeon like that.'

'I get you,' Mr McAllister said. He leaned forward to tighten the laces on his trainers. 'Well, you've certainly picked a dignified name,

Darryl. The Pawnee are a deeply spiritual nation – proud, and largely peaceable, too. Unlike many Indian tribes, they never waged war with the United States. In fact, they were loyal servants of the army and highly sought-after as trackers and scouts. Had a real nose for a trail, they did. Particularly good with horses, too. There's a wonderful story in one of my books about a Pawnee brave who calmed a wild stallion by talking to it.'

Suzie shivered. 'I couldn't do that. Horses scare me a bit.'

Too right. I'd always been terrified of them. When I was six, Gran had taken me to Belvoir Castle to watch a medieval jousting display. Afterwards, in the castle courtyard, the knights had come in, still on horseback. I'd just taken an apple from Gran when suddenly a horse's head came over my shoulder and snatched the apple straight out of my hand. Everyone had laughed out loud. But I'd turned in fright, looked up at those slavering, crunching teeth and immediately shouted to be taken away. I'd avoided horses from that day on.

Suzie thankfully changed the subject. 'Were Pawnee warriors dead fierce, Dad?'

'Oh yes,' he said, reclining his chair. 'Men of legendary mettle, they were. The tribe was made up of four main bands. The dominant band were the Skidi, which means "wolf". Suzie, pass me that book with the green spine, would you?'

Suzie slid a book off a shelf beside the fire. Her father thumbed a few pages, then showed the book to me. 'Pawnee flag – top left, as you look. Red wolf's head over a tomahawk and peace pipe. They signify war and peace; the wolf is a symbol of cunning and courage. Believe me, if you saw that flag you knew you were in for a bit of a scrap.'

'Who with?' I asked. If they didn't fight the army, who did they fight?

'Other Indians,' Mr McAllister said. 'There was no love lost between certain tribes.'

Suzie surfed the rug to come and have a look. 'Is it true they scalped people, Dad?'

He bent forward and lifted her pony tail. 'From here, where it's longest,' he said to me, chopping a hand round the back of her head.

'Da-ad! Do you mind?'

'The Indians believed the hair was the soul, because it continues to grow throughout life. The taking of your enemy's hair meant his soul was rendered earthbound and hence no threat to the spirits of your ancestors. This gave you "strong medicine" – great power over him. The Indians had a special system for recognizing acts of war, such as scalping. They called it "counting coup".'

'Coo?' I said, thinking he meant the noise pigeons made.

He spelled it for me. 'It's a French word, roughly translated as "war count". The more scalps or weapons or horses you took, the more respect you earned from the tribe. The day a man counted his first coup was the day he became a true brave. There were many true braves among the Pawnee. They were well-noted for their guts and endurance. Even faced with the worst adversity, they would never give up.'

'And neither will you by the sound of it.' Mrs McAllister appeared in the doorway. 'Tea's ready. In you come.'

We all filed into the kitchen and took our places around the table.

Over tea (Quorn fillets with salad; not bad) we talked about more general things. But, inevitably, the subject came round to pigeons.

'Tell us what you have to do at Lenny's,' said Suzie.

So I went through my list of jobs: disinfecting floors, scraping down perches, sweeping loose feathers, washing out drinkers, topping up grit trays, mixing up corn—

'Ah,' Mr McAllister interjected, expertly chewing a cob of the latter, 'part of the Pawnee's staple diet. Corn was considered a sacred gift. They saw it as a sort of symbolic "mother".'

Mrs McAllister drummed her fingers. 'Well, Helen, symbolic "corn" of Suzie, would like her to pass the butter, if she would.'

As the dish came across the table, Mr McAllister dinked it with a knife. 'And that is true Pawnee.'

'The butter?' queried Suzie.

'Its shape,' said her dad. The surface of the butter had been scraped into rolls. 'You couldn't miss a Pawnee Warrior. They took their hair back in a horn like that and held it in place with buffalo fat.'

'Ewan,' Mrs McAllister muttered.

Mr McAllister ate his tea.

For pudding there was ice cream and strawberries. After two helpings, Mr McAllister made his apologies and said he must 'fly' to the health club he managed. I thanked him for his help and said I would always think of my Pawnee as being peaceful but very courageous, now.

'Racing will be his test,' he said. 'With a name like that, he'll fly till he drops and won't ever give up. Wouldn't mind a bob or two on him, come race day.'

With that, he said his goodbyes. As Mrs McAllister turned to the dishwasher, Suzie asked, 'Mum, can we go to my room and play some music?'

'Don't have it on too loud,' was the response. We'd already gone by then.

Suzie's room was twice the size of mine (you could actually *see* some open floor space; unwashed clothes covered most of mine). As I sat on the bed (next to a dinosaur nightie case) she suddenly whirled on her heels and exclaimed, 'Aw, got a great idea!' She dashed across the landing into the bathroom, returning with a tub of blue hair gel.

'No way,' I said.

She grinned, opened a drawer of her dressing table and pulled out a shallow plastic box. Face paints.

'No,' I said.

'Come on,' she laughed. 'It'll be fun. You'd like to be a Pawnee warrior, *wouldn't you*?'

She did my hair first. She combed my fringe upright, smothered it with hair gel and rolled it back – round one of her mum's rollers! To cover our giggles she played a CD. Then she began to cover me with paint. She used brushes for strokes and fingers for smudges. Fifteen minutes passed before she stood back, grinning. 'Cor,

Preston was right about fearsome displays of colours. No-one's gonna touch you, looking like that.'

I whipped round and faced the mirror. It looked like a firework had frozen on my face. 'You're for it,' I said and turned to grab her. She squealed and leapt onto the bed. I got her round the waist and pulled her to her knees.

'Darryl, get off! I think you look great! I can throw you any time I want to, remember!'

'Try it,' I said – and tickled her like mad.

'Agh!' she squealed.

'*Woo-oo-oo-oo-ooh!*'

'Aw, *Darryl*! Don't *tickle*!'

'*Woo-oo-oo-oo-ooh!*'

She bounced around to face me, panting with laughter, loose hair plastered across her cheek. She brushed it away with the back of her hand. 'Honest, you look dead cool,' she whispered.

The bed sagged, bringing us closer together. She walked two fingers up my arm. 'You warrior; me squaw,' she breathed. Our foreheads touched. Our noses met. Our heads began to tilt to opposite sides. My lips were a layer of gloss from hers – when the door swung open and her mum walked in.

'Ermmmm?'

Suzie leapt back like a scalded cat. 'Mum, you might have knocked!'

'I did,' Mrs McAllister said brusquely. 'I couldn't make myself heard for the whooping and the music.' She switched the CD off. 'Gemma's on the telephone for you.'

Suzie threw me a serious look. 'Could be *angel* business,' she mouthed.

'*Warren?*'

'*Yeah.*'

We swept downstairs.

'It's me,' she panted into the phone. 'Did you find anything? Cool! Spill.' There was a pause, she clamped the mouth-piece a moment. 'Gem says Fern's cousin, Brad, used to go to a youth club with Warren. He knows who Laura is.' She picked up again. 'Soz? How do you spell it?' She wrote the name down: *Laura Graveney*.

'She's crackers about Warren,' I heard Gemma gabble. 'She goes with him, even though he cheats on her loads.'

'Ask about Laura's sister,' I hissed.

'Was that Darryl?' Gemma squawked.

'He came for tea,' said Suzie. I couldn't help noticing the smirk on her face.

'Suzie McAllister, you tramp!'

I snorted with impatience and leaned into the

phone. 'Get on with it, Thomson. What else did Fern find?'

Suzie listened a moment then reported: 'Her sister's name's Felicity. She's fourteen and podgy.'

'What did she have that Warren wanted?'

Suzie exchanged a few umms. 'We don't know.'

My heart sank. For a moment, I thought we were going to crack it. Then . . .

'Yeah, could be useful,' Suzie yattered on. 'Yeah, I know it. That posh place up on Waverley Road?' She lowered the receiver. 'We know which school they go to.'

I took a mental walk up Waverley Road, to the part where the road split off and there were always conkers on the ground in the autumn. The only girls you ever saw there were dressed in boaters and red-maroon blazers. I pictured the sign on the wall by the gates. Bright gold letters on a dark blue board.

SPENNER HILL SCHOOL FOR GIRLS.

CHAPTER TWENTY-FOUR

'Spenner Hill?' said Gazza. 'That's Duck Egg's school. Felicity Thingy must be in her year group. Wow. Inside info. You gonna ring her? Duck Egg, I mean?'

I sighed and lobbed a tennis ball at Superman's head. With the assistance of the bedroom wall he nodded it perfectly back to my hands. 'Oh yeah, and what am I going to say? Excuse me, Susan, do you know if Felicity Graveney's got anything that might kill pigeons? She'd think I was nuts.'

'Gemma could do it,' he said with a shrug. 'Girls are dead cool about stuff like that.'

I swung sideways into a sitting position. 'Gazza, don't tell *Gemma* about Susan.'

'Oh yeah,' he sighed, with a hint of snideness.

'Don't want McRat to think you're two-timing her.'

I bounced the tennis ball off his head. 'Suzie's cool. Don't call her that. I can't two-time her, we're not going out. We're just mates, OK?'

He slumped back against my beanbag, not OK. 'You've gone dead weird just lately. All you wanna do is talk about *Susans*. Why don't we play footie any more?' He flicked a rogue Subbuteo player under my bed.

'Gazza, I need to find out about Warren.'

'*Well, ring the Duck Egg then!*'

He was spitting now, and I couldn't blame him. He was right about Susan – but I just couldn't do it. I'd never told him I'd invited her to Lenny's loft or how angry she'd been when I let her down. That door was too scary to open up again. I put my trust in my 'angels' instead.

I checked in with Gemma and Suzie every day, hoping they'd have more clues to the puzzle: *what had Felicity Graveney got that Warren Spigott was so interested in?* But after their promising start, the angels could find nothing new on the sisters. Time slipped by. Days grew into weeks. The trail, like an unwanted egg, went cold.

Suzie reckoned Warren had tired of the game,

and wouldn't risk another crack – since he'd been exposed. Warren and Felicity were history, she said. I should just forget it.

But the mystery wriggled like a worm in my brain. I couldn't shake off the nagging feeling that Warren was merely biding his time, and that somehow he knew my every move.

Bogeyman. *Ugh*. He made my flesh crawl.

Then, one day at Lenny's, I made a sort of breakthrough. It had nothing to do with Felicity Graveney. It was just plain Warren.

And dead plain creepy.

It happened on the day of Pawnee's first training toss.

'The graveyard,' said Lenny, nodding towards St Barnabas. 'Always like to start my young 'uns there. Nice wing beat for them, across the fields. Fetch a basket. I'll grab the little Indian.'

Heart pumping, I opened the narrow shed that formed one end of the smaller loft. It was stacked to overflowing with pigeon rammel: drinkers, troughs, all sorts of gubbins. The wicker baskets Lenny used to carry pigeons to his club were wedged in near the top of the pile. I tugged one out and pushed the door to, only to find that something had snagged along the bottom edge: a photograph – of Warren, holding a pigeon. Crouching beside him was the woman whose picture I'd seen in the lounge. I'd never asked, but it had to be his mum.

'Haven't seen that for a bit.' A wisp of cigarette smoke rolled across my shoulder as Lenny came to join me by the shed. He tipped his ash and took another drag. 'He'd be about twelve when that was taken.'

Twelve. He looked happy. It didn't compute.

Lenny read my scowl. 'I know what you're thinking, but he loved the birds then. That hen he's holding – bred it himself. He named it Little Elf, after his mum. Emily Louise Frances Spigott.' He ran a nicotined finger down the woman's hair. 'What do you think?'

'She looks nice,' I said. Curly black hair and a wide warm smile. It was easy to see where Warren got his looks.

'I was lucky to catch her,' Lenny said wistfully, handing me Pawnee in exchange for the photo. He thumbed it fondly, straightening a corner. 'There's not many would let themselves fall for a bloke who's devoted most of his life to pigeons. What about the bird? Remind you of any?'

I studied Little Elf. She had a bold, round eye and blue-black markings. 'Cherokee?'

'Aye. She's Barney's mum, and your hen's gran.'

And Pawnee's *great*-grandma. Wow.

Lenny tilted his head. 'One day I'll show you my book of matings. Half the fun of this sport is trying to breed champions.' He put the photo in his shirt and smiled at me then: a boy and his treasured pigeon. A pigeon descended from one his wayward son had bred. I shuddered inside and felt as if a ghost had walked right through me. For a moment, I could have been Warren.

'Come on,' said Lenny, 'let's make a start.'

We put Pawnee in the basket and set off across the open fields, on a path that snaked like a stream bed through the crops. There were a zillion things I wanted to know. Was Warren's mum dead, for instance? If she was, what had happened? And where was Little Elf? Why wasn't she in the loft? Strangely, in the end it was *my* mum we spoke of. Halfway to the church Lenny asked how she was.

'Annoyed,' I said, ''cos she can't get into her jeans. She was sick last week, but Gran says it's normal. She's going for something called a scan next Friday.'

'Let's hope they find a baby, not a squab,' joked Lenny, 'or Dad's going to hit the roof. Talking of squabs, how were Clara's today?'

Clara, one of his stock breeding hens, had not long hatched a pair of young. 'Fine,' I said. 'Mr Spigott, did you ever find out about Cherokee's eggs? That second lot Dad brought over?'

'Still undergoing tests,' he said. 'I'll tell you when I know for certain.'

We climbed a low stile and crossed into the grounds of the church itself. Gravestones sprouted out of the grass, birds sang happily in the sanctuary of the trees. Lenny opened a gate onto a tarmac path. We followed it past a marbled memorial and into the shade of a huge oak tree. Just beyond the tree, out in the light again, Lenny stopped and rested the basket on a grave.

IN MEMORY OF EMILY LOUISE FRANCES SPIGOTT, BELOVED WIFE AND DEVOTED MOTHER.

I gulped. One question answered.

'Training's a lot to do with habit,' said Lenny, slipping the buckles on the basket front. 'I've had young 'un in here a lot this week, just out in the garden, schooling him to fly from the basket to the loft. He soon cottoned on to what was expected; they usually do if they know there'll be food on the landing board. All he has to do now is apply it over distance. Ready?'

A sudden rush of dread made me splutter out loud, 'He won't fly away, will he?'

Lenny looked back towards the estate. 'If he takes it into his head to go, there's nowt we can do to stop him, lad. But he'll get back. My grandma's budgie could home from here. All we want to see is how quickly he learns.' He let the flap of the basket fall.

For a moment, nothing happened. Then a blue, speckled head stretched warily forward and a copper-bronze eye viewed the new surroundings. Pawnee took a hesitant step towards freedom. He squatted, did a dropping, then took to the air.

He beat a path almost vertically upwards, then veered off erratically towards the church spire. At first I thought he was going to whizz round it, as if to perform the 'slingshot' manoeuvre that spaceships sometimes did around planets. But at the sight of stone he quickly changed course, then zipped away over the fields.

Lenny passed me a pair of small field glasses. 'Follow him through these. Look for the lofts. He'll be there in a flash.'

I put the glasses to my eyes. The roofs and chimney pots of Station Road loomed into blurry, goggle-eyed vision. I found the ivy-clad wall of number 16, the tall French windows and finally the lofts. Lenny had dropped the long wooden shutter that made a landing board for the homing traps. As I brought it into focus, Pawnee touched down. He pottered forward, into the nearest trap, and disappeared inside the loft.

'He's in!' I cried.

Lenny lit up a fag. 'Aye. Straight as an arrow. He's Little Elf's line all right.'

I lowered the glasses, hesitant; pondering.

'What?' asked Lenny. His eyes were like searchlights.

I couldn't help myself. I had to ask: 'Mr Spigott, what happened . . . to Little Elf?'

He tipped his chin and blew a funnel of smoke. 'Can't say without telling you what happened to Emily.'

I glanced at his tattoo. The dripping heart. 'OK.'

He nudged a stone with his toe. 'One springtime – it would be four years ago now – Emily took a basket of birds up the motorway, to let them loose on a training toss. The air was bitter cold and rain was forecast, but she went – at my bidding – 'cos the old 'uns were slightly behind with their work.

'On the way home the weather took bad. She was coming to the bridge that spans the River Bake when a juggernaut skidded out of control. It clipped her, forcing her through the barriers. Front of the car collapsed like a sock. It hit the Bake and sank. Took two hours to crane it out, as long again to cut her body free. She was dead before she hit the water, they said.

'When the police came to tell me there'd been

an accident, I was here, in the garden with Warren. I didn't need telling. I already knew that something was up.'

'How?' I asked. My gut was churning.

Lenny dropped his cigarette and stubbed it out. 'The birds came home; Emily didn't. Little Elf, who'd always trapped like a good 'un, sat on the loft roof, spooked about something. Warren tried to talk her down, but she wasn't having any. All she did was sit. I think she knew – about Emily, I mean. I can't explain how; just something in the air. When I heard, officially, about the crash, I went up the garden and tried to explain it gently to Warren. He couldn't – or wouldn't – take it in. All he would say was, Little Elf needed to trap. Over and over and over he said it. We had to get Little Elf in.

'I coaxed her down the next morning, after I'd exercised some of the others. Warren insisted on going to see her. I let him be, thinking he needed the bond. I didn't smell the smoke for another ten minutes.'

'Smoke?' The word came up on a wave of panic.

'Those lofts in the garden are new,' he said, picking up the basket and walking away. 'Warren burned the old one down.'

CHAPTER TWENTY-FIVE

Suzie sat back with a hand across her mouth. *'He killed his own pigeon?'*

'Loads of them,' I said; 'they choked on the smoke.' I joined her at the kitchen table. 'Barney Knowall escaped. He got drenched with water when a drinker shelf collapsed, and that's what saved him. He flew out when the roof caved in.'

Suzie shook her head in disbelief. 'How could anyone do a thing like that?'

I shrugged a bit coldly. 'Warren blames Lenny for his mum's accident. Lenny says Warren has never forgiven him.'

Suzie hugged herself tight. 'Are you going to tell your parents?'

'Can't. Mum might be upset.' She'd been sick again that day and was having a lie down at Dad's insistence. They'd argued about it, loudly but briefly. Everyone, even Grandma Thornton, seemed anxious about Mum's coming scan.

'I think your dad would want to know—'

'Know what?' he said, breezing in from the hall.

Suzie eyed me quickly and knew she had to cover. 'We were talking about . . . training Pawnee, Mr Otterwell. I was asking Darryl if he'd told you about it.'

'Hardly ever says a word,' he said. He plonked two mugs and a teapot on the tray. Tea for him and Gran. They lived on the stuff. 'How's he doing, then, Darryl?'

So I told them how he'd performed in the graveyard, and what was coming next. 'We have to let him go from further and further off, so he builds up his muscles and learns to home properly.'

'Sounds sensible,' said Dad, spooning sugars. 'How long before he can race?'

'Ages,' I replied. 'We're going to put him in a come-back race.'

Dad's eyebrows hooked into a frown. 'Aren't they all "come-back" races? Isn't that the point?'

'Dad,' I tutted, rolling my eyes. 'Races get longer throughout the season, but for the last couple of weeks they come back to shorter distances so the birds won't get too exhausted.

We're going to train Pawnee for a race from Taunton; that's about a hundred miles.'

'Wow,' said Suzie, looking impressed.

'Dad, can I go to Mr Spigott's on Friday, after school? He wants to show me how to basket up birds for race nights.'

He raised a single eyebrow at Suzie. 'In other words, "Dad, can I have a lift, please?"'

Suzie fluttered her lashes at him. 'That's what dads are for, Mr Otterwell.'

He shook his head, grinning like a soppy rabbit. He loved it when Suzie cheeked him like this. She had him completely taped. Mum had warmed to her now as well, though she often complained it was Suzie's fault for encouraging Natalie to 'swear like a trooper'. 'Sausages' had gone from Nat's vocabulary. Suzie had taught her a new word: 'Sherbet'. 'Sherbet Fizz!' if she was really narked.

'I suppose so,' said Dad, feigning his favourite put-upon voice. He picked up the tray. 'I'm glad it's going well – with the birds, I mean.' He threw a proud glance at me and a thankful one at Suzie. She'd helped me through some pretty bad moments, he knew.

As he drifted down the hall the doorbell rang and Suzie pressed my fingertip with hers. 'He's right, you know. It *is* going well. Perhaps you

179

shouldn't tell about Warren, after all. I say we forget him and just—'

The doorbell went again.

'Darryl?' Dad shouted, cutting Suzie off. 'My hands are full. Get that, will you?'

'I'm nearest,' said Suzie. She scooted down the hall and yanked the door open.

A long cold breeze swept into the kitchen. Then a voice like an insect, spitting acid. 'Who are you?'

Susan Duckins.

I dived into the hall.

'Who are *you*?' Suzie echoed, bristling with defiance.

A slow smile broke on Susan's face. I could tell she lapped up challenges like this. 'I'm a vampire,' she answered, shaking her hair. 'I've been invited in before. That means I can cross your threshold, *ta*.' Arms folded, in she came. 'Hi, Darryl.'

'Hi,' I gulped.

Dad's face came round the front-room door. 'Who is it? Oh. Hello, Susan.'

I glanced at Suzie. Her face had suddenly turned pale and anxious. She closed the door on auto-pilot.

Susan smiled at everyone in turn. 'Hope I'm not interrupting anything?'

Stone-faced, Dad said, 'I think you three had better go out, or at least talk quietly in the kitchen.'

Susan voted with her feet. 'Been out, thanks.' She flounced past me and into the kitchen.

Suzie, head down, followed her in. Dad caught me and gave me a dark, stern look. 'I hope you know what you're playing at, Darryl?'

Playing at? What was that supposed to mean?

I shrugged him off and followed the girls. They were sitting as far apart as they could get; Susan perfectly relaxed on a chair; Suzie on a stool in the corner, by the door, hunched up tight and chewing her hair. Claws at five paces. That's what it felt like. Suzie eyed Susan. Susan eyed her – trainers, jeans, top (labels), face, figure, face again, hair. I was amazed she didn't demand a twizzle.

'I'm not staying,' said Susan, 'as you've got company. It's boring in Spenner Hill on a Sunday.'

'Why have you come to visit?' I whispered. Pathetic. Suzie knew it and scowled.

Susan clicked her tongue. 'A little bird told me you were taking your pigeon to Lenny's after all.'

I started. How did *she* know that?

Reading my confusion she quickly answered,

'Must have been Grandad, I s'pose.' She straightened her fingers and hurred on her nails. 'So I thought I'd ask if I could still, y'know, go. After all, you were *bursting* to take me once.'

I felt as if the life force had been sucked out of me. Suzie, her hand curled into a fist, was shaking gently, knuckling her lip. I had to do something, fast. 'Can't,' I said. 'I go on Friday nights now.' A half lie. It didn't improve things with Suzie, and it only brought Susan Duckins to the boil.

'Tops. Even better. That means I get to see Flick in town on Saturdays. So, is it a "date" then, Darryl? Next Friday, at Lenny's? I know he lives in Barrowmoor. What's the address?'

Before I could speak, Suzie, unexpectedly, asked a question: 'Do you go to Spenner Hill Girls?'

The iciness of it made me shudder. What had made her want to know *that*?

'Top set,' Susan boasted. 'Why? Where do you go?'

'Is Flick in your class?'

Susan threw me a tired look. 'She run the school quiz or something?'

I shook my head. I had no idea why Suzie wanted to know these things, and Susan, patently, didn't care. She put her hands behind her head and stretched to expose several inches of her waist. That was the limit for Suzie. She stood up and left the room.

I pegged her in the hall. She brushed me off, cold.

'I'm sorry,' I hissed. 'I didn't know she was coming. She's Mr Duckins' granddaughter. She helps with the pigeons, that's all. I'm not going out with her or anything.'

Suzie blinked and ran a fingertip under her eye. 'It was her on your workbook, wasn't it?'

A simple 'yes' could have saved me, but I didn't have the strength or maturity to say it. I looked away instead. Bad, bad move.

'I have to think about some things,' said Suzie, and was gone.

I got rid of Susan five minutes later, after she'd made me promise to ring Lenny and ask for permission to take her over. A promise twice broken was a sin, she said. And her grandad so wanted her to help me out. I wasn't going to let *him* down, she hoped.

When she'd gone, I went out to the shed. My head felt numb. My senses, stewed. I mucked the birds out in a total daze.

I was coming towards the kitchen to fill their drinker, when I overheard voices through the open window: Mum (now up again after her rest) and Dad, having one of their 'meaningful chats'. Mum said, 'You're joking! Both girls? Together? What was madam doing here?' She meant Susan, of course, or 'Miss Trouble', as she was popularly known on Planet Mum.

Dad reached for a tea-towel and started drying pots. 'It certainly wasn't to warm up the hall. I could have lagged the pipes, it was that frosty. Maybe she's keen on him?'

Mum responded with a tidy *pff*! 'Wake up, Tim. He's too young for her. That was always one-way traffic. I don't trust that girl. She's got her own agenda.'

Agenda? I thought. What does that mean?

Natalie piped up: 'Mummy, is Darryl going to marry Mizz Trubble?'

'Certainly not,' said Mum. 'And it's time for your bath. Run and find Grandma; I'll be up in a minute.'

Natalie pottered out of the kitchen.

'So you reckon the birds are the attraction?' asked Dad.

Mum ripped a piece of kitchen towel off the roll. 'If you think that floozie's here for the pigeons, you're even dafter than he is.'

And with that she followed Natalie out of the kitchen.

*   *   *

I couldn't understand what Mum was saying. If Susan wasn't here because of the pigeons and I was too young to go out with her, what other reason could she have for coming? I figured it hinged on the word 'agenda'. In the lounge, after tea, I asked Gran what it meant.

'It's a list of things to be done,' she said, notching down the TV sound.

Susan had a list of things to be done? That didn't sound right. But Gran hadn't finished.

'But to say someone "has their own agenda" is what's known as a euphemism – that's a way of expressing something bad in a gentler manner. Why, who do you know who's got an agenda?'

'No-one. Just tell me what it means – please?'

She took a tissue from her sleeve and blew her nose. 'It means the person concerned is up to something. Acting for themselves. Scheming, if you like.'

'Scheming?' I repeated. *Susan was scheming?*

Grandma Thornton nodded her head. 'It means they have a plan,' she said.

CHAPTER TWENTY-SIX

I needed Garry. I needed football. I needed *boy* things all around me. The world of girls was too complex and scary. How did dads survive all this? How did they grow up liking girls, marrying one and not getting totally boggled in the process? Gazza was right. All girls were *weird*.

I brought him up to speed at school the next day. We were lying on the grass in the playing field, looking up at the sky, having a 'cloud race'.

'Plan?' he said with reference to Susan.

'I don't know what it means,' I tutted. 'I don't care either. I just wanna sort things out with Suzie.'

'No chance,' he said. 'You're totally chilled.'

Too right. She'd blanked me all morning. The angels had avoided me as if I had 'frost zone' stamped across my brow. On the way into

Preston's class, Suzie had gone past chatting to Fern as if I was a dummy in a high-street window. And during IT, when Mr Anwar had asked her to hand out worksheets, I'd tried to be polite and say 'Thanks' for mine and she'd simply replied with a civil, 'You're welcome' and moved straight on to Connor.

'Gazza, will you talk to Gemma?'

'What about?' he said. 'My cloud's winning.'

'Suzie, you bone.'

He put his tie in his mouth and blew it out again. 'After the way she looked at you at break?'

I sucked in sharply. Gemma's first glance at me that morning had seemed to express every boy-hating phrase in one pulse of her pupils: *pig, toad, scumbag, creep, two-timing heap of useless . . .*

The bell went for the end of dinner.

'Just mooch, OK? Try and find out what Suzie's thinking.'

'That's easy. She thinks you're rubbish. She only dumped you yesterday. Your cloud's stopped, by the way.'

Yeah, I thought. Just like my life.

I was missing Suzie like mad already.

But they wouldn't talk to Gazza. Not about me. He reported in the toilets later. 'It's useless. They just go "Bong",' he said. 'I ask them a question and as soon as they know it's for you they say "Bong!"'

'They're mental,' I said, hurling a paper towel into the bin. I swung on my heels, facing the cubicles.

'No doors,' said Gazza, rushing round in front of me.

'They can all get stuffed,' I yelled into his chest.

'You can never be mates with a girl,' he said. 'Hols next week. World Cup. Footie!'

Yeah. Footie. That's what I needed.

Girls. They were such a pain.

The situation didn't improve all week. As we approached the long summer holidays I was sure that one of them was bound to say something – send a vom-coloured letter at the least.

Nothing. Total silence. Struck right off the angel register.

The worst of it was, my body wouldn't do what my brain was telling it. Despite my irritation, I couldn't take my eyes off Suzie in class. It got so bad that in our last science lesson Mr Preston made me sit at the front so I wouldn't be 'gawping at Miss McAllister like some pathetic, lovestruck puppy'.

The class laughter was the turning point. I decided I hated her after that. I thought ahead, to my 'date' after school, to Susan Duckins, who was *drop-dead gorgeous*. All through science I transmitted that thought to 'Miss McAllister' with all the telepathic power I possessed. Suzie merely yawned and looked away.

To really twist the knife, Mr Preston made me recite back chunks of the lesson. It was all about genetic mutations. Soooo *boring*. Bug-eyed monsters from the planet Grubblemuck might have been something worth listening to. Instead, I got to write this in my book: 'How do subtle changes in genetic disposition help animals adapt and evolve?' Something to ponder over the summer. I couldn't wait to get started – not.

It didn't help that things were bad at home that night. Every kid except me had left school, buzzing. I trogged down our drive feeling empty and dissatisfied – and stumbled on Dad, smoking a cigarette.

My dad didn't smoke.

'What are you doing?' I muttered.

'Having a quiet think,' he said. He blew smoke from his nose like he'd done it for years, tapped some ash into a nearby planter. I couldn't cope. I shrugged and walked on.

'Darryl?'

'What?'

'Don't give your mum any grief tonight, eh?'

Then I remembered: today was Mum's scan. I hurried inside to find her.

She was in their bedroom, in Gran's arms, clutching a tissue, weeping gently. On her lap was what looked like a polaroid photo. I watched through the crack in the door as she stroked it once and said to Gran, 'Oh, Mum. How are we going to cope?'

Gran rocked her like she was a little girl. 'We'll see it through together, like we always do.' She moved the photo onto the bed. 'Come on, bathroom for you. Darryl is going to be home any minute.'

Mum blew quietly into her tissue. 'I don't want him to know till nearer the time.'

'If he asks, I'll tell him everything's fine.'

I slipped into my room as they came to the landing. On the click of the bathroom door, I tiptoed into Mum and Dad's room.

The photo was still on the bed. It was an odd-looking picture, black and white, a bit like a lampshade viewed side on or a time-lapsed photo of a pendulum, swinging. At the centre of the 'shade' was an oval-shaped cave. Mum's womb-thing, I guessed. At the base of the womb was a dark grey shape. It took me a while to work out it was a baby.

But it wasn't a normal baby. I knew it was only a few months old and its hands and feet would be stubby and weird – a bit like the wings on a growing pigeon. But it wasn't the hands that made me swallow. It was the baby's head. I could make out a chin and a twig of a nose, but the crown of its head was totally wrong. It was far too big, as if it had a lump or a swelling or a blister.

Bug-eyed monster from the planet Grubblemuck.

Mum had a mutant growing inside her.

CHAPTER TWENTY-SEVEN

No-one wanted to talk about it. I asked Mum, before tea, if the scan was OK. She said the hospital doctor was pleased with her progress and it was very thoughtful of me to ask. Did I want burgers or pizza tonight?

I tried Gran, outside, while she was pegging washing. She said Mum was slightly more pregnant than expected, but it was a common condition and I wasn't to worry. How was Suzie, by the way? We hadn't seen her much lately.

I avoided all queries to do with McRat and asked outright: was it going to live?

Grandma touched my cheek. Yes.

On the way to Mr Spigott's, I tackled Dad. I hit him with the question Mum had asked Gran: how are we going to cope?

Not surprisingly, he winced. 'A new addition

to the family inevitably brings its fair share of challenges, Darryl – particularly financially.'

We flashed past the Barrowmoor sign. 'Do you mean it's going to need special care?'

He looked at me oddly. 'All babies need special care. What time am I picking you up?'

'You don't have to; Mr Spigott's bringing me home from his club. Can you drop me here, please?' We were at the turn to Station Road.

'Why?' he asked, looking puzzled.

'You always moan you can't turn round on the estate.'

He raised an eyebrow, but I didn't care. He'd never be able to lower it again if he saw Susan Duckins leaning on a pillar box just around the curve of Station Road.

She was there, waiting, as we'd arranged, her bike lying in the gutter at her feet. She greeted me with all her usual charm. 'What you gawping at?'

Her outfit. Tight black trousers; purple sweater; hair frothing out of a clam-like grip; earrings falling like miniature wind chimes. She looked *awesome*.

'Darryl, shut your gob. People'll mistake you for the pillar box. Which number?'

'Sixteen.'

She nodded and touched her hair. 'Good. Bring my bike.'

Mr Spigott met us at the garage. All week I'd been dreading this moment, wondering how he'd take to Susan. But for once, she was on her best behaviour. She greeted Lenny with a whopping smile and thanked him politely for inviting her.

'Aye, well,' he said, looking her up and down. 'A Duckins is always welcome here. You'd best avoid the garage; it's a bit of a tip. Go through the house. Front door's open.'

'Ta,' she said, and stepped inside.

'By 'eck,' Lenny whistled as soon as Susan was out of earshot. 'How did an ugly old crust like Alf have any say in producing that? Bit overdressed for handling pigeons, but at least there's nothing mucky to do. Are you and her . . . ?'

I shook my head. In my dreams, maybe.

He nodded. 'Put the bike away.'

I chained it in the garage and hurried to the lounge. Susan was admiring Lenny's paintings. 'This flighty's really good,' she said, pointing to a bird with a single white feather in its outstretched wing. 'Is it one of yours, Mr Spigott?'

'No,' said a voice, 'it was one of mine.'

Warren.

He walked in, drying his hair with a towel. He was stripped to the waist. No shoes. No socks.

He threw Susan an arrogant glance. Her earrings tinkled as she tossed her head.

'Can't you make yourself respectable?' said Lenny.

Warren ran the towel along the length of his arms. He wasn't as muscular as I'd always thought, but when did a snake ever need brute strength? 'If I'd known we had royalty coming,' he said, 'I'd have clipped my toenails specially, Dad.'

He pulled a comb from his jeans and turned to the mirror. Amazingly, Susan kept her cool. Warren hadn't even looked at me.

Lenny sighed and stabbed the keys of an old computer. A piece of paper spewed out of a printer. 'Race sheet,' he said, seeing me looking. 'I'll explain when we're at the loft. Come on, lass.' He beckoned Susan towards the French windows. She put her chin in the air and followed him outside.

As I slotted in behind them, Warren had a pop. 'Enjoying the birds then, Darryl?'

I looked over my shoulder, at his reflection.

'Nice hen,' he sneered.

And spat on the mirror.

At the top of the garden my 'hen' was making a big impression. 'You've got a lot of widowhood boxes, Mr Spigott. How do you rate those sputnik traps? Do you fly South Road? North? Or both?'

'Your grandad's taught you well,' glowed Lenny. He answered her questions with a generous smile but never once tried to humour her. I felt a mild tweak of rivalry mounting, especially when she took the race sheet from him and asked, did he want these basketing up? I was the pupil, not *her*.

Lenny showed me the sheet. It was divided up into a sort of grid, a bit like a football coupon. On the left was a column of pigeon ring numbers, with the colour and sex of each bird written in, then several smaller columns headed 5p, 10p, 25p, 50p, £1, £2 and £5 next to that. Under some of these headings, crosses had been marked. I quickly worked out that the crosses were to indicate which birds Lenny was betting on.

'These are my entries for tomorrow's from Weymouth.' He ran a finger down the list of numbers. 'Find each bird, check it over carefully, then pop it in the basket if you think it's OK. Then we'll take them to the club for marking up.'

Susan immediately raised a hand. 'I can't go to your club, Mr Spigott. I'd like to, but I have to be somewhere else later.' And out came another whopping smile. I'd never seen her like this before. So nice. So friendly. So . . .

I blushed as Lenny caught me looking at her.

For the next half-hour we did as instructed. I collected up the pigeons; Susan checked them over for damaged flights. We didn't exchange much, other than pigeon talk. But that was how I wanted it. Relaxed. No tongue-ties. This was what I'd dreamt of so many times. Being here, close to her, sharing the birds. If she had a 'plan', this had to be it. I'd be part of her agenda any time.

As we basketed the last bird she smiled at me and said: 'Meant to ask you, Darryl: how's . . . ?'

'Pawnee?' I looked at Lenny. He nodded his consent. 'In here,' I gabbled, backing through a door into the young bird compartment. Pawnee was on his usual perch, two up from the bottom row. Despite losing his last few strands of down and looking every bit the perfect pigeon, he was still way down the 'pecking order'. I gathered him and handed him over to Susan.

'Dark chequer,' she murmured, 'with a speckled head.'

'Do you like him?' I wanted her to say he was the best she'd ever seen.

'He's skinny,' she said, thumbing his neck. She tipped his foot to examine his ring. 'Treble four, double eight. Nice and easy to remember.'

'Yes,' I said. 'Why did you want to read his number?'

She handed him back. 'Just checking he's legit.'

She smiled again, thinly, and waltzed into the garden.

After a brief discussion we put the pigeons in Lenny's car and wheeled Susan's bike back onto the drive.

'Ta for a lovely evening,' she said.

'My pleasure,' said Lenny. 'Come again, any time.'

My heart thumped. Any time. *Yes.*

'I'd like to,' she said. 'I—' She broke off, catching movement to her left. Warren was watching from the bay window. 'Better go,' she beamed. 'Bye, Mr Spigott. Bye, Darryl.' She leaned over her bike and pecked me on the cheek.

Warren's eyebrows clashed like daggers.

And it wasn't my blushes he was frowning at.

I couldn't concentrate on pigeons after that. I wasn't really there at Lenny's club. When people spoke to me – and everyone did – I made 'suitable noises', as Mum would say. Lenny drove me home for quarter to nine. On the ride back he asked, 'Where were you tonight?'

'Pardon?' I said.

He turned the radio down. 'Your mind – it wasn't on marking up pigeons.' He threw me a sideways glance. 'That girl, Alf's granddaughter – I don't mind you bringing her round. She's an able lass; she knows her stuff. But you're at my place to learn about birds. Do you know what I'm getting at?'

I nodded. He knew I'd been thinking about her. Not difficult. I couldn't *stop* thinking about her. She'd kissed me, right in front of Warren. I couldn't get over the way he'd looked. Totally envious. I'd like to see his reflection now. *Nice hen, Darryl.*

Yeah, all mine.

'Go on,' said Lenny, pulling up outside our house. 'I'll see you tomorrow. I've arranged a twenty-mile training spin for the little Indian. We'll time him in together, eh?'

'Great,' I said. I opened the door and swung myself out.

'Oh, and I've got a surprise for you, too.'

'What?'

'It can wait till morning,' he said. 'Give you something else to think about, won't it?'

Versus Susan? Huh. No contest.

I let myself in and called out so everyone would know I was home.

Dad stepped out of the lounge. 'Darryl, can you come in here, please.' His voice was low, his face expressionless. Surely he hadn't found out about Susan? It didn't sound like his telling-off voice.

He waved me to the sofa. I sat beside Gran, who was doing a crossword. Mum was in her usual chair by the fire. The TV was on, the sound turned down.

'I'm afraid we've got some rather bad news,' said Dad.

I looked at Mum's tummy.

'Not me,' she said.

'You had a phone call while you were out,' said Dad. 'From Susan Duckins' mother.'

My face went ghostly pale.

'She was trying to find Susan and wondered if you might know her whereabouts. I told her I didn't think you would, as you'd gone to Mr Spigott's.'

'Is Susan all right?'

Dad took a deep breath. 'This isn't about Susan. It's about her grandad.'

Alf? I looked at Mum.

'Mr Duckins has died,' she said.

CHAPTER TWENTY-EIGHT

His heart packed up. That's what they told me. Conked out in his sleep. No better way to go.

I couldn't take it in. It was strange knowing that the man who'd helped with Cherokee, the man who'd given me Gregory Peck, the man who, in a way, had brought Sioux and Pawnee into this world, had now gone out of it.

Grumpy old Alf.

I was too stunned to cry.

'The funeral's on Wednesday morning,' said Dad. 'At that church near Mr Spigott's house. Susan's mother has said you're welcome to attend. I've left the decision open, of course, but if you'd like to be there, Grandma has offered to chaperone you.'

'It's your choice,' she whispered, resting her pen. 'It's not everyone's cup of tea – a burial.'

'You don't have to think about it now,' said Mum.

But I already had. I wanted to go, to take him a feather. Susan, too. She was going to be mega-upset.

'Oh, there was something else,' said Dad. 'You had another call – a girl . . . Gemma someone?'

Thomson? What did she want?

'You're to call her back before nine, if possible.'

I glanced at the clock: 8.55.

'Go on, you might just catch her,' said Gran.

I dragged myself to the phone.

'Left it late, didn't you?' Gemma grumbled.

'Didn't know you lot were talking to me.'

'*I'm* not,' she growled. 'I think you're a rubbish two-timing toad. Fortunately, Suzie's prepared to forgive you.'

'Stuff off, Thomson. I don't—'

'We know about Felicity Graveney.'

A muscle twitched in my shoulder.

'Suzie guessed last week, but we needed proof.'

'What's she got?'

'I'm not allowed to say,' she peeped, enjoying it. 'You've gotta meet us on the park. One o'clock, Tuesday. Suzie wants to tell you face to face. I hope she ties you in a knot and throws you in a bin. You're gonna be dead sick, Snotterwell. You'll wish you'd never dumped on her . . .'

I felt like a caged wolf, totally wired. Pacing. Turning. I couldn't sleep. I couldn't talk it through with Gazza, either. He'd gone to see his gran in Wales that weekend. My only relief was visiting Lenny's. Saturday was brilliant (no Warren, thank goodness). Pawnee had been taken to Westcotes Hill, nineteen miles due south of Barrowmoor. His first real training toss. I was terrified at first. What if he didn't come back? What if he hit a power line somewhere? What if a peregrine falcon got him?

Lenny laughed out loud. 'What if Santa Claus catches him and stuffs him in his sack? Stop fretting, lad. He was born to home. Anyway, Alf'll look out for him, you'll see.'

Sure enough, at twenty-three minutes past ten a clutch of birds appeared above the fields. All had returned home, safe and sound. Third in, of six, was Pawnee Warrior.

That wasn't the only spark of joy. As soon as the returning youngsters were settled, Lenny asked me to transfer Clara's fledglings into the young bird section. 'What do you think?' he asked.

'I like the ash-red flighty,' I said.

'Hmm, very pretty – ah, which reminds me.' He dipped in his pocket and pulled out an earring. 'Found it on the lounge floor, Friday night. Will you ring her – or me?'

I must have looked so, so hungry. He grinned and handed it over. 'I want names for these fledglings,' he said. 'They'll need to be entered in my book.'

'They're your squabs, Mr Spigott.'

'No, they're not,' he said. 'They're the second batch from your hen.'

Cherokee's eggs? But I'd thought—

He smiled and tapped his foot. 'You'd be amazed how long an egg survives. Nothing wrong with your home birds, lad. You were just unlucky to lose that squab. I hope this makes up for it. Now we've got three potential champs.' He offered me a hand.

I shook it, hard. 'Thanks, Mr Spigott.' I was almost in tears.

'Names, by next Saturday,' he said. 'And nothing I can't spell, either – OK?'

At the time it had sounded really great. More birds. More little Indian names. But next Saturday was still another week away. There was Tuesday on the park before then . . .

I found them on the bench beside the bowling

green. Gemma, Suzie . . . and Garry Taylor.

My best mate, Gazza.

Hanging out – with *them*.

'It was their idea,' he tremored, standing up. 'I'm not siding with them, honest. They just know some things. You've gotta listen, Darryl. This is mega.'

'Park it,' said Gemma, tugging him into line. 'You're here for us, in case he gets nasty.'

I homed in on Suzie, staring me out with those soft brown eyes.

'Sit,' she said. She pointed to a stone just opposite the bench. There was a brass plaque on it, words of peace. I wasn't feeling peaceful. I dropped a shoulder, stood.

'Fine,' she said, sighing. 'Be big and tough. Here's what you wanted to know: remember when I was at your house – and *she* turned up, Susan Duckins—?'

'Tart,' muttered Gemma.

'Don't,' snapped Suzie. She pinned me again. '—and she said her best mate was someone called Flick?'

'So?' I sneered, tilting my head.

'It's short for Felicity,' Garry spouted. 'Y'know, *Felicity Graveney*? That's what Warren meant in the bogs when he said there'd been an interesting development. Laura's kid sister turned up with – *a friend*. It was Duck Egg. *She's* his secret weapon.'

'Get lost,' I shouted, backing off. 'You're all mental.'

'No,' said Garry.

'You're making it up 'cos none of you like her . . . and *she's* just jealous!'

I stabbed a finger at Suzie. She folded her arms and looked away.

'He's a big-headed pig,' said Gemma. 'I told you he'd be like this.'

Gazza came to me then. I pushed him off. 'Stay with your girly friends, OK?'

'Smack him one, Garry.'

'Shut up,' he told Gemma. There was no way Garry would ever fight me. I'd been beating him in play scraps since Year 1. He turned to me, pleading. 'Fern Summers lives near Barrowmoor. Last Friday she walked her dog round Warren's estate, spying – for them.' He nodded at the fallen angels. 'Fern says she saw a girl who looked like Susan going into Warren's house—'

'Big surprise,' I hit back. '*She* knew we were there.' I pointed at Suzie again.

Garry shook his head. 'Fern saw you leave. But Duck Egg came back all on her own. Warren let her in. She's going with him, Darryl. It's not a joke.'

No. It wasn't a joke. 'Stuff off,' I shouted, kicking blindly at him. 'I saw Susan with Warren that night. He called her, and she totally *blanked* him.'

'She's playing games,' snapped Gemma, 'so you won't suspect. She's using you as an excuse to be round at Warren's. Lads, you are sooo stupid.'

'You're the STUPID one!' I screamed, and lashed at her.

She squealed and rolled away with her hands to her head. Suzie leapt up and twisted my arm. 'Touch her and I'll put you down,' she said.

I looked into her face. Her eyes were streaming.

'She lost an earring,' I said. 'She probably went back to look for it, that's all.'

Her bottom lip trembled and she pushed me away.

'I hate you!' I shouted. 'All of you!'

I stamped on the peace stone and didn't look back. I wouldn't have seen much of them if I had.

My eyes were streaming, too.

CHAPTER TWENTY-NINE

Wednesday morning. Funeral dress. They made me wear the suit I'd been bought for my Uncle Jamie's wedding. Mum spent ages brushing the jacket, tugging the sleeves down over my shirt cuffs, worrying about the length of the trousers. I tried to tell her it didn't matter. Alf was dead. He wouldn't be concerned about me looking smart. I wasn't going to church like a scarecrow, she said. (She even checked that my *underwear* was clean.)

On the bus to Barrowmoor it drizzled with rain. Gran fished out a brolly, but we didn't need it. By the time we arrived at St Barnabas Field the sun was parching the morning mist, throwing a rainbow over the fields. We arrived at the church to see Alf's coffin being slid out of a hearse. It took six men to shoulder it into the chapel. One of them was Lenny Spigott.

Keeping our distance behind the other mourners, Gran and I found a pew at the back. The seats were hard, unpolished, cramped; the spines of the hymn books broken and threaded. Organ music wafted from a speaker on a stand. Mortar crumbled from the bare grey walls.

They laid Alf's coffin on a pair of wooden trestles, with the head of the box towards the altar. Lenny walked backwards down the aisle, bowing his head before he turned. He was dressed in a slim-fitting suit and tie. He took a place three pews from the front, bunching in beside some pigeon fanciers I'd met at his club. I scanned the front rows for Susan Duckins, but couldn't see her for the press of bodies.

A vicar with two wings of hair above his ears took his position in the pulpit. We sang a dreary hymn, then the vicar spoke: 'We are gathered here today to commemorate the life of our friend Alfred Duckins.'

Alf, he said, had been a faithful husband, a caring father, a devoted grandfather. Friends knew him as a charitable fellow. A bear, perhaps. Brusque. Austere. But a kind and deceptively *tender* man – never more so than in the devotion he'd shown to his cherished pigeons. I swallowed hard and looked down at my feet. Gran pushed a tissue into my hands. We sang another hymn, even worse than the last. Then Susan stood up and read from the Bible. She spoke in a clear voice and didn't crack once. She was dressed in a tight-fitting knee-length suit, sensible shoes and a wide-brimmed hat. Gran nudged me and whispered, 'Doesn't she look beautiful?' She was gorgeous. A shining black angel. Stunning.

As the service came to an end, the coffin bearers moved forward again. Alf's casket was carried back down the aisle. Relatives and friends filed past, two deep. Susan, in tears now, clutching her mother, dabbed a hankie to her eyes and didn't see anyone. Mrs Duckins breathed me a silent 'hello'. When the family had gone, Gran touched my arm and we shuffled out last.

Sunlight glistened on the daisies and weeds. The occasional raindrop dripped off the trees. We passed the headstone of Emily Spigott, on the way to a plot near the railway embankment. The bearers laid Alf's coffin on the ground, on top of two wide canvas straps. In the earth beside the coffin was a deep, neat hole. Bright green matting had been laid out around it. 'To stop your shoes getting muddy,' Gran explained. We gathered and listened to the vicar once more: 'Ashes to ashes, dust to dust.' With the aid of the straps, the bearers lowered Alf to his resting place. Several people wept. Some dropped soil onto the coffin lid. I pulled two feathers from my jacket pocket: one from Cherokee, one from Greg. I floated them into the grave. 'Thank you,' I whispered. 'For helping with my pigeons.' I looked up through a film of tears.

Susan was watching me.

Before I could speak, arms enclosed her, drew her away.

'Come on,' Gran whispered, linking arms. 'She'll talk when she's ready. She needs her family now.'

We walked slowly back to the church. On the driveway, relatives and friends of Mr Duckins were hugging, chatting, clasping hands. People, young and old, moved to comfort Susan. My chance came as her mother turned away to chat to the vicar.

'Be sensitive,' Gran whispered. 'Gentle condolences. She's in a delicate state, remember.'

I took a deep breath and moved towards her. She was dabbing her eyes and didn't look up. I was halfway there when she jerked rather stiffly and her hand went into the pocket of her suit. She turned her back on the whole congregation and clamped a mobile phone to her ear. 'Where?' she said, and glanced around, frowning. Her thumb touched a button. The mobile beeped. She looked quickly at her mother (still deep in conversation), then backed away towards the church.

She didn't go in. She veered away round the big stone urns and slipped down the path leading back through the graveyard. Then she ran like a girl who had a purpose in running, with no idea I was following her. She pulled off her hat, flicked out her hair, hopped briefly to adjust one shoe. As she neared the grave of Emily Spigott, she threw herself forward like a girl in love. A pair of arms were waiting for her.

Who else could they belong to but Warren Spigott?

She stood on tiptoes and kissed him, hungrily. He bunched her hair and pulled her off, laughing. 'No,' she complained, pushing forward for more.

That was when he looked up and saw me watching. I staggered backwards, colliding with a headstone. Warren pulled Susan into his chest, patted his mouth and made a silent whoop.

For a moment, my breathing stopped. Then the world closed in with a rush, and I ran.

I swept across the graveyard, not knowing where I was headed, or why. My knees began to bend as I hit a steep rise. My breath started coming in painful bursts. My feet squelched into the soft, wet earth. At the peak of the railway embankment, the sudden giddy emptiness almost snatched my consciousness away from me. The knock of a goods train woke me again. I stumbled forward, slipped on my bum, slithered, rolled, got my hands stung, caught dead bushes in the sweep of my limbs. I tumbled towards the railway sleepers, fell a short distance, hit hardcore. My heels kicked against click-clacking stones. There was oil in my nostrils, dirt on my knees, steel in my ears, betrayal in my heart. I leaned back and an engine rattled past me.

I was six feet away from death.

When Lenny Spigott put his hand on my shoulder and tore me into his heaving chest, some dark part of me was ready to know what it would have been like to be under that train.

Lenny cupped my face in his trembling hands. 'What in God's name has he done to you?' he whispered.

Hollowed me like a Halloween pumpkin.

I was dying from the inside out.

CHAPTER THIRTY

Lenny guided me to his car. He avoided the church and its outlying grounds, knowing there would only be awkward questions. He put a blanket around me that smelt of wicker, went back for Gran and drove us home.

He spoke alone to Mum on the step. He seemed flustered, too shaken for a cigarette even. I heard him telling Mum he didn't know what had happened, but that Warren had been in the graveyard with Susan and that seemed to have sparked something off.

'Susan.' Mum spoke her name with frost on her breath.

'I have no idea what's going on,' said Lenny.

There was a pause, then Mum said, 'Goodbye, Mr Spigott,' and closed the door quietly in his face.

That was the start of the worst day in my family's history. Mum rang Dad, argued on the phone, wept when he told her he couldn't leave work. When Gran tried to comfort her, even they bickered. When Natalie wouldn't stop asking questions, Mum screamed and threw a cushion at my sister's head. All day long. Non-stop.

When Dad came in, it hit a new peak. In the lounge, he demanded the whole story. I didn't even open my mouth. Gran said what she'd seen, what Lenny had done.

Dad got off on the wrong foot entirely. 'So Warren hasn't touched you, then?'

'For crying out loud, he doesn't have to *touch* him!' Mum was into orbit right away. 'That boy is depraved. He's playing mind games. He's got to be stopped.'

'Kissing a girl is hardly a crime.'

Mum looked at him darkly. 'He set Darryl up – deliberately – to provoke him.'

Dad found a tortured frown. 'We can't prove that. All Warren has to say is Darryl was in the wrong place at the wrong time.'

Mum threw up a hand. 'I don't believe I'm hearing this. Why are you defending that thug?'

'Oh, now you're being utterly ridiculous.'

'You think it's ridiculous that Darryl ran

blindly to a railway cutting and nearly got himself maimed – or killed?'

Dad grasped the back of his neck. 'That's an over-reaction.'

'Don't patronize me,' Mum said angrily. 'I've listened to this nonsense long enough. I'm tired of character building and stiff upper lips. I will not have Darryl near that boy again. I'm not going to see him systematically destroyed by that . . . that evil swine.'

'Claire, you're not looking at this rationally!'

'He's my son!' she screamed, red-faced, arm thrusting. 'How rational does it need to get? He's my flesh and blood. Just like this!' She pointed to her tummy. 'Why don't you just condemn this now and let's get it over with?!'

That was it. I couldn't stand any more. 'STOP IT!' I yelled, covering my ears. 'Just stop arguing. Everyone!'

And before they could catch me, I'd run to my room.

It seemed like half the night, but it was probably no more than half an hour before Mum came up.

'Hey,' she said quietly, caressing my shoulder. I was lying on my side, facing the wall.

'I'm sorry,' she whispered. 'We're all so busy screaming at each other. No-one's stopped to think about you. Will you talk to me a minute?'

I nodded, silent.

She ran a soft hand over my head, carefully placing my hair behind my ear. 'Your dad and I have had a civilized discussion. We think it would be best if you could be away from this for a while, so you can have a little rest. Grandma has suggested that she takes you up to Yorkshire, to give you a change of scene. What do you think?'

I ran a knuckle under my eye. 'Who's going to look after Cherokee and Greg?'

'I know the routine.'

'But what about Pawnee?' I grabbed a pillow and buried my face.

'Hey,' she went, rolling me over. 'Pawnee's safe at Mr Spigott's.'

I shook my head. 'Susan read his ring number. She'll tell Warren he's there. He'll kill him.'

Mum took a decisive breath. 'I'll have your dad call Mr Spigott tonight. If anything happens to that bird, I'll see that Warren goes to court for it.'

'He won't care, Mum; he burned down his dad's loft once.'

She shuddered at that, but her mood was unforgiving. 'He didn't have me up against him before. Come on. Come down and have some tea. I promise you, there'll be no more shouting. In a couple of days, this will all fade away. I think a spell in the Dales will do you good. I wouldn't mind going myself. It's tiring, carrying what feels like a couple of puddings around in your tum.'

She pushed herself up and walked to the door. I could have left it, but I had to ask: 'Mum, will it be *really* deformed?'

'Pardon?' she said, and sat down again.

'I saw that picture, after your scan. It's got a big head, hasn't it? The baby's a mutant, and no-one wants to talk about it.'

A moment passed while she worked it out. Then she bit her lip and stroked my arm. 'Oh, Darryl.' She looked at me as if she could burst. 'It's not a mutant, love. What you saw was a healthy scan – of one child, with another lying behind it.'

She smiled as I took this in.

'Another? How can there be another?'

'It's normal,' she whispered, 'if you're carrying twins.'

CHAPTER THIRTY-ONE

Gran lived in a village called Ducks Halling, on the eastern edge of the Yorkshire Dales. Dad always called it 'Ducks Quacking', 'cos the odd duck-call was the most exciting thing that ever happened there, he said. As a kid, I'd played commandos in the corn, picked fruit from the hedgerows, fished for sticklebacks in the stream. I'd even sat on the gate of Westwell Farm and watched loose horses grazing in the fields. Warren Spigott had not existed for me then. He was still a shadow behind the wardrobe. I could never have imagined that because of him I'd be going back to Gran's as a runaway one day. That's how I felt when I told Mum I'd go: a deserter, looking for a hidey-hole.

The first few days passed by in a blur. There were twenty-six cottages in Ducks Halling; no bus stops, one post box and an old-fashioned telephone kiosk that no-one ever seemed to use. The nearest shop was four miles away. Top activity was dragging a twig along the hedgerows. I did a lot of dragging that first week in Yorkshire. I did a lot of thinking, too – mostly about *her*, Susan Duckins; the way she'd dived into Warren's arms, their kiss, his whoop, my brush with the goods train. Over and over, round and round. The endless spinning numbed my senses, making a black hole in my brain. A hole for darker thoughts to tumble into. What if Susan, for instance, had killed little Sioux? Sent me to fetch a glass of water and . . . ? All at the snap of Warren's fingers. She was a slave to him now, as I had once been.

Warren's secret weapon.

Now and then Gran talked to me about it, while we were pruning her plants, perhaps, or putting out the tea, or walking through the blue-bell woods near the cottage. Gentle coaxing. That was her way. A problem shared. A shoulder to lean on. Gradually, I opened up. I told her how I felt betrayed by Susan, and stupid 'cos I'd bagged off Gazza and Suzie. It hurt to know that Warren had won. Gran said Warren hadn't won, and I shouldn't blame myself for the hurt he'd caused. He would get his just desserts one day. My task was to let go and try to move on.

One night I got a call from Lenny Spigott. He rang at the time Mum normally did, which threw me a bit and made me nervous. He opened up with news about Warren. 'He's not going back to school next year. Never was one for exams and such. Says he's off travelling with a couple of mates.'

'Um,' I grunted. Warren gone. I should have felt elated. Instead it seemed meaningless.

'Young Indian's doing well,' he went on. 'Had him flying fifty miles these past two weeks. Clocking up some good times, too.'

'Oh,' I said.

I thought I heard him draw on a fag. 'I'm still looking to put Clara's squeakers in my book.'

Names. He still wanted names. I gritted my teeth and blew a hard sigh. From the corner of my eye I caught Gran watching. She had a strangely concerned look on her face. She put some knives into a drawer, smiled and went out.

'Aye, well, no rush,' said Lenny.

'No,' I agreed, and we said our goodbyes. I put the phone down and the television on. I curled into a chair with my head on the arm.

I didn't want to think about pigeons.

I knew this was worrying Gran. The very next day she tried the happy routine. If I wanted to go home, I only had to say. Gosh, I must be anxious to muck out the pigeons. Catch up with Gazza. Kick a football round the park. She was trying to reel me in, like an astronaut in danger of drifting into space. I heard her on the phone to Mum that night. Gloomy, she reported, I was getting gloomy. At one point I thought I heard her whisper 'depressed'.

That weekend, Mum and Natalie came up.

Mum jollied me from the very first moment she arrived. I was hugged. I was tousled. I was talked to a lot. She'd driven up, so I was taken out, too. We did a theme park, the pictures, a tram museum, a cable car ride, several picnics in the Dales. We had a holiday of sorts. Family time. But everyone knew we were counting down the days till the moment Mum told me I had to go home.

In the end, it didn't come the way I'd expected. What happened took everyone by surprise. On the Saturday morning, a week after Mum had arrived with Nat, my sister wanted to feed some ducks. Gran found a spare crust and handed it to me. Take Nat down to the stream, she said.

So we went hand-in-hand (at Mum's insist-ence), searching for the famed 'black mallards' silhouetted on the roadsigns at the borders of the village. It was strange holding hands with Natalie. I never did it at home, it was far too embarrassing. But here, in the sleepy quiet of the village, it was comforting to feel her gripping my fingers. We followed the stream towards Westwell Farm. It was there, at the gate, that Natalie broke free.

'Horsey,' she said, and ran there, pointing.

'Nat, come on.' I walked on a pace, bored.

No answer. I turned. The gate, which had never been more than a wafer, was skewed away from the bottom of its post.

My sister was in the horse's field.

'Nat!' I shouted. 'Nat, come back!'

She was running in her bumbling, loping style, pigtails bouncing off her shoulders. Far across the field a chestnut horse stood sideways to her, watching her approach. Suddenly, Nat put her foot in a hole and fell forward, awkwardly, on her face. The bread went up in the air. She yowled in pain and started to cry.

'Nat,' I gasped. My heart walloped.

The horse clicked into a trot.

I scrabbled over the gate and ran, trainers thumping on the soft, lush pastures. I reached Nat's side and tried to make her stand. She fell back on her bottom and bawled for Mum. I knew then that I would have to carry her out. But in the time it would take me to pick her up and go, the horse would be right on top of us.

Panting hard, I turned to face it. It stopped within easy clod-throwing distance and let out a brief inquisitive snort. I half-wondered if horses could read our minds. If they could, this one would know I was praying, clinging to a looping fragment of speech I'd heard one time from Suzie's dad. The Pawnee were wonderful with horses, he'd said. One had calmed a stallion by talking to it.

I didn't talk. I couldn't manage that. And I knew that a sudden cry for help might panic the horse and make it rear. So I stared instead – taut, unblinking. I must have looked like a scarecrow to it, my arms angled in a Christmas-tree shape, fingers stiffer than spokes in a wheel. The horse snorted again and tossed its head. Flies buzzed on its nose and mane. It smelt of straw and leather and sweat. It turned an ear and looked at me uncertainly. Then it rolled its eyes towards Nat. I stepped sideways to cover her. The horse jerked back. Its posture was proud, but its nerve had cracked. I pictured my face in Suzie's mirror. Painted brave. Pawnee warrior. I put a war whoop into my head. The horse turned submissively towards a barn. Then it spun on one hoof and cut away.

I picked up my sister and carried her to the gate.

There I was met by Mr Gill, Gran's neighbour, out with his dog. He offered to carry Natalie for me. But Natalie screamed to me not to let go. She clamped on like a koala bear. With every bump on the short walk home, one of her tears ran down my neck.

Mum was frantic. 'Horse?' she said, and had to sit down. Gran wrapped some ice cubes into a towel and pressed it gently against the swelling. She was pretty sure Nat had only twisted her ankle but thought we should take her to the hospital to be sure.

Natalie wouldn't go without me.

'You're her hero now,' Gran whispered.

'All I did was stand there,' I said.

Gran squeezed my hand, the same way she had so many years ago in the courtyard of Belvoir Castle. 'It takes a special kind of courage to do what you did. Not everyone possesses it, Darryl.'

I thought about Warren Spigott then. If he had been in my shoes, would he have faced the horse?

Gran smiled and touched a hand to my face. We both knew that the moment had come – to make a stand of a different kind. I nodded and took Nat into my arms.

Hospital, first.

Then home.

Then Warren.

CHAPTER THIRTY-TWO

When I told them, Mum went white with shock. 'No, Darryl. I absolutely forbid it.'

Dad lowered his paper and stared at me thoughtfully.

'I want to see Pawnee. I want to check he's OK.'

'Then ring Mr Spigott. You're *not* going to Barrowmoor.'

Dad's first effort was tame and short-lived. 'Claire—?'

Mum swatted it on the first breath. 'He's not going. That's final. End of discussion.'

'You can't stop me,' I said.

That almost cost me Dad. 'Don't get cocky,' he warned.

'Dad, if I don't go, Warren will win.'

'It's not about *winning and losing*!' snapped

Mum. She threw down a duster and sank into a chair. 'Men: you're all so . . .' She couldn't or wouldn't find the words.

Dad's eyes continued to probe me a moment. Then he glanced at Mum and gestured me towards her. I knelt down and slid one hand across her tummy. 'Mum, please. I love Pawnee. If I don't go, I'll never see him again. People always say you should stand up to bullies. This is the best way, isn't it, Dad? Just carry on as if nothing's changed?'

He folded his paper, slowly, into four. 'I'm sorry, Darryl. I can't take sides.'

I squeezed Mum's hand. 'Please let me go. He's my pigeon, Mum. *You* kept him alive – while he was still in his egg. I can't desert him, can I? Please . . .'

My first idea was to go in through the back. Arrive by St Barnabas. *Bong*. On the hour. I thought it would spook Warren if he was there, to see me wander in, unexpectedly, from the garden. But as I biked up to Barrowmoor I changed my mind. To do this properly, I had to be bold. Sneaking in would be what Dad would call 'a hollow victory'. I had to look at Warren as just another horse.

So I chained my bike to a Station Road lamp-post and walked up the drive with my head held high. A window was open upstairs in Warren's room, a cricketing commentary tumbling out of it. I cast off a shudder and rang the bell, long enough for someone up the garden to hear. I heard Warren shout: 'Da-ad! Door!' But no-one came. I rang again. There was movement in the house. Shuddering stairs. The lounge door banged. The front door blipped with the change of pressure. Warren's outline appeared behind the glass.

Whoosh.

'Yeah, what do you—?'

His face went through a range of expressions: surprised, suspicious, thoughtful, smug. But not angry. That threw me. He should have been angry. Annoyed that the toe-rag had dared to return.

'Well, look what the sewer's thrown up.' His mouth curled into its usual sneer. He folded his arms and leaned against the door frame, shining a boot against his calf. He glanced at my hands. I had no weapons and my fists weren't clenched. I didn't want to send him any sort of signals.

'I've come to see your dad.' I got it out without a fumble.

He looked me up and down. I looked *him* up and down. He didn't like that. He straightened up and called me a cocky little—

'I'm not scared of you,' I said. I'd practised that with every pedal push from home. I tensed up, wary that he might lash out. And in a way he did. He hit me with the deadliest blow of all: something totally unexpected.

'Fair enough – you'd best come through.' He opened a hand towards the lounge.

Now I was truly scared. Why would Warren invite me in? He was up to something. Why wasn't he *angry*? 'Mr Spigott!' I called. 'It's me, Darryl!'

'He's up the garden,' said Warren, beckoning me through. He pushed the French windows open for me. 'Go on. Go and see him. He's expecting you, I think.' He grinned coldly. 'Game on, Darryl.' He marked the air with a finger, then climbed the stairs, whistling.

I went in like a secret agent, checking the shadows for any sign of movement. The atmosphere was odd, as if someone had died. I made it to the windows and sprinted up the garden, knowing I could always escape across the fields.

As I reached the gap in the privet hedge, Lenny stepped out of the small stock loft. 'Darryl?' he spluttered. 'Where did—?'

'Mr Spigott, I want to carry on,' I panted. 'I've come to see Pawnee.'

I saw a lump pass down his throat. My knees

began to wobble. Something was wrong. He shot a suspicious glance towards the house, wondering, perhaps, what Warren had said. He reached for his cigarettes and looked at me squarely. He eyes were so pale, frozen almost.

'Mr Spigott, what's the matter?'

He stepped forward and turned me away from the loft. 'I've something to tell you, and it's not very pleasant. I'd have called mid-week, but there was still a chance then . . .' His words trailed off into an agonized sigh. He removed his cap and rubbed his forearm over his brow. 'Wednesday evening, I took some young 'uns training. I sent eight up. Only five came back. Young Indian wasn't among them.'

I staggered backwards, into the hedge. A thousand bits of privet pinned me upright.

Lenny grimaced. 'I'm sorry, lad. These things happen. I'm as choked as you are. That bird's a real favourite.'

'Warren,' I said, gasping for breath. Now I understood the reason for his smugness.

Lenny shook his head, blowing smoke in an arc. 'Not this time. Yesterday I took a call from Cheltenham, from the offices of the Association. Someone had rung a bird in. It was dead and ripped open – probably the work of a bird of prey.'

Ripped open? My stomach took an awful lurch. 'What colour was it?'

'A blue,' he said quietly. 'One of the others.'

'Where *is* he, then?' I shouted. 'Where's Pawnee?'

Lenny looked distantly across the fields. 'Missing,' he said. 'Your bird is missing.'

CHAPTER THIRTY-THREE

I couldn't bear it. I had to tell someone. Suzie's was the only place I could go.

Her father answered the door. 'Darryl! Thought you'd taken a canoe up the Platte.'

I looked at him gone out.

'River in Nebraska; Pawnee homeland.' He batted me indoors with a rolled-up paper. 'Helen, look who's here.'

Mrs McAllister came in through the kitchen, wearing a pair of gardening gloves. 'Hello, Darryl,' she said. Her tone was cold. She knew about Susan. It was there, in her eyes.

'You'll be wanting Suzie, no doubt,' said Mr M, clearly unaware of any sort of bust-up. He called upstairs. She came pounding down, stopping halfway when she saw who it was. She glanced at her mum. Mrs McAllister pulled off her gloves as if she wished they were really my arms. She frowned and went into the kitchen.

'Hi,' said Suzie quietly.

'Hi,' I muttered, not sure where to look. I homed to her knees, poking through the rips in her denim jeans. She pushed up the sleeves of her lemon-coloured top.

'Can I talk to you?' I said. 'Gazza's gone to Cornwall.'

She flicked her hair and stared at the wall.

Her dad merely reeled back, looking puzzled. 'What sort of a question's that? Go on, up you go. She's been as miserable as mud while you've been away.' He winked and batted me towards the stairs.

Suzie turned in silence and headed for her room.

I told her everything. About Alf's funeral. Susan and Warren. How I'd nearly hit the train. Mum and Dad rowing. Going to Gran's. Facing the horse. The prospect of twins. 'I've had to move out of my room,' I said. 'Into the box room, where Gran was. They're building a new room, over the garage. It was s'posed to be a surprise for me, when I came back. But it's taking longer than the builders said.'

She nodded politely, all the while playing

with the ends of her hair. 'Is that *all* you came to say?'

I shook my head. 'Pawnee's missing.'

'Darryl,' she snapped. 'You might at least say sorry for— what do you mean, missing?' She looked up, concerned. Whatever rift we'd created had healed in an instant.

So I told her about my trip to Lenny's and how I'd tried to face off Warren. 'He's killed him,' I said. 'I know he has. He only let me in 'cos he knew what his dad was going to tell me. He planned it all.'

Suzie shook her head. 'That doesn't make sense. He just saw an easy chance to hurt you, that's all. Like he did with Sioux. He could have heard about the birds from his dad, any time.'

'Well, why did he say "Game on"? That means we're still playing. That means it isn't *over*.'

'Darryl, that's what he *wants* you to think. Making you feel confused and frightened is what gives him such a hold on you. You're playing right into his hands. It'll never be over if you carry on like this.'

Suddenly, the frustration got too much. I snatched up her hairbrush and slammed it on the bed. 'I *know* he did something. I'm gonna kill him.'

'With a plastic brush?' Suzie sighed and rested back on her forearms, pinching up little clumps of her duvet. 'We've got to stay cool and think this through. What else did Lenny say?'

I stood up and paced around, restless. 'He said the main reason birds go missing is that they follow other pigeons into towns and stuff. He was hoping Pawnee had flown off course to another loft. But if that had happened he'd have heard by now.'

'What about birds that get attacked by predators?'

I folded my arms like a mummy in a tomb. Why did she have to go and say that? It reminded me of Preston and his stupid rock doves getting picked off by peregrine falcons. 'If they're lucky, they come down injured in a field. Strong ones recover and still fly home. Mr Spigott said a bird came back after three months once.'

'There,' she said, her voice full of hope.

'Suze, he was telling me to make me feel better. He thinks Pawnee's dead. I know he does.'

'Darryl!' Her eyes were firing now. 'If there's a chance Pawnee could make it, he will. Remember what Dad said about the tribe?'

'It's just a name. He's not a real Indian.'

'He's a champion,' she insisted. 'He's tough, like Cherokee. You didn't give up on her when her wing was broken. Come on, Darryl. Fight for him. And I don't mean with a hairbrush, either.' She yanked it from my hand. 'If you honestly believe that Warren did something there's only one way you'll ever find out: go back and pretend you've accepted it. Don't let him scare you off. Try and show him that *nothing's* going to faze you. That'll make him mad and he'll have to react. Sooner or later, he'll make a mistake.'

Go back? My head fell into my hands.

Suzie smoothed her hair back and tied it in a band. 'I'll help you – promise. So will Garry and Gem.'

I sank down, not knowing what to think. 'What if we find out Warren *did* kill him? What are we going to do then?'

She teased a lock of hair off the prongs of the brush and rolled it between her thumb and fingers. 'Imagine this was black, jet-black, like Warren's.'

I shrugged and told her I didn't get it.

Slowly, she gathered my hair into her fist and tugged it back till the roots began to hurt. She put her mouth to my ear. 'Woo-oo-oo-ooh.'

'You're kidding?' I said.

She chopped her hand round the back of my head.

No, not kidding.

Scalp him.

Wow.

CHAPTER THIRTY-FOUR

At first I didn't believe her. She'd always said fighting was not an option – and hacking off Warren's precious hair qualified as major scrapping, no question. Even so, the thought of it toughened my heart. I growled and said Gazza would go for his boots. He really hated Warren's boots. Dead showy, he called them. Suzie said no problem, we'd have the boots, too; we'd stuff the hair into them and throw them in the cut. It's all of us now, she said. Me, you, Gem and Garry.

And she said it with a fighting glint in her eye.

I left her house in a mixed sort of state. Part of me wanted to go up to Barrowmoor and call Warren out right there and then. But I couldn't hold onto the feeling for long. By five that evening I was aching again, crushed by the gnawing sensation of loss and the terrible helplessness of simply not knowing what had happened to my bird.

Somehow, I held it together at home. When they asked, I told Mum and Dad I'd seen Mr Spigott and he'd said it was cool for me to start again next Saturday. I didn't say anything about Pawnee. I knew it would only upset Mum, and I just couldn't handle the fuss right then. So I kept myself to myself that night. After tea I stayed out with Cherokee and Greg. Played games on my computer. Went to bed.

The next morning Suzie came round so early Dad answered the door in his dressing-gown. He shouted up to tell me my 'lark' had arrived. Not funny, under the circumstances.

Suzie's plan was to hang with me as much as she could, to avoid parent hassle and keep my mind focused. We had a bowl of soggies, then went out on our bikes. We didn't do much, just sat around and talked. She knew I was pining about Pawnee. I kept swinging from being OK one minute to screaming it was so unfair the next. Suzie was cool. She let me mooch if I wanted, made me ride my bike if I had to burn energy. We tried not to talk about pigeons too much, but one day, on the park, this came up:

'I need to think up some Indian names.'

'Why?'

I explained about Cherokee's second batch of eggs. I was thinking if Pawnee really had gone, there could at least be others: his brother and his sister.

'I know what Dad would choose,' said Suzie. 'When I was little, he used to call me his Comanche Princess, 'cos Mum used to braid my hair a lot.'

Comanche Princess. I told her I liked that.

She put a kiss on my cheek, making me wince. 'Darryl,' she huffed. 'No-one's *watching*. Some boyfriend you're gonna be.'

'Sorry. What about the other?'

'Choctaw,' she beamed, after a pause.

Choctaw? It sounded like a word you shouted when you'd won a board game of the same name: *Choctaw!*

'Dad's got this old-fashioned record,' she said. 'He likes it 'cos it's about someone called Billie Joe McAllister who lives near this place called Choctaw Ridge. Dad's brothers are called William and Joseph, and McAllister's our surname, and Choctaw's an Indian tribe. So, Comanche Princess and Choctaw Ridge. There – am I a genius or what?'

'Write them down,' I said.

'Darryl! What did your last servant die of?'

'Tickling,' I said.

She grabbed a pen.

One afternoon, some five days after I'd seen Lenny Spigott, I biked to St Barnabas' church with Suzie. I showed her Emily Spigott's grave and pointed out the lofts in Lenny's garden. I took her to the field the birds flew over. She cupped her hands above her eyes and stared due south. 'This is the way he'll come, then?' she said.

I told her she was dreaming.

'Don't give up,' she said.

But in my heart I already had. By the time we got home for tea that night I told her I couldn't hold out any longer and I had to tell Mum and Dad everything; sorry. She nodded in silence and said she understood. She'd help me, she said. We went into the house.

We met Dad on his way downstairs, cleaning a paint brush in a newspaper wrap. In the absence of a holiday (because of the twins), he'd taken time off work to decorate my room. 'Darryl, you're to call Mr Spigott,' he said.

Suzie's head came up.

I gulped, 'What about?'

He looked at me as if I'd left my brain on my bike. 'Pigeons, I should think.'

'Darryl, what do you want for tea?' Mum called.

'Dunno,' I shouted. I couldn't face food. I felt sick. What was Lenny going to tell me? They'd found Pawnee like the other pigeon? Torn apart by a bird of prey?

Suzie lifted the phone and put it in my hand.

Mr Spigott came straight to the point. 'I've just returned from a loft in Derby. Your bird's been found – alive.'

I almost dropped the phone. 'He's not dead,' I breathed.

Suzie flapped her arms and danced for joy.

'Is he OK?'

'Aye,' said Lenny, though I could sense reservations in his voice.

I didn't press it. 'Can I come and see him?'

'If you're quick. I'm out at eight.'

'I'll hurry. Can I please bring a friend, Mr Spigott? Not Susan. My proper girlfriend, Suzie.' I looked at her and blushed.

He paused, then said. 'This won't turn out like the last time, I hope?'

'No chance,' I said.

'Aye, all right. Don't dally, OK?'

I told Mum we'd get chips on our way to Barrowmoor. We didn't. We went straight to Station Road.

'Peculiar business,' Lenny said. 'Fly-overs like this aren't uncommon; birds often get lost in bad conditions. But it was sunny that day and no wind to speak of. He's always been straight as a crow before.'

I looked down at Pawnee, nestling in my hands. Suzie ran a thumb across his speckled neck. 'Could a falcon have chased him away?'

Lenny sucked on a fag. 'If he'd met a falcon, lass, he'd be dead.'

'He's got dried blood on his feet,' I noticed.

'Aye,' said Lenny. 'Chap at Derby treated a cut. He thought the bird had caught on a power line at first, but there are marks on his ring – as if someone's tried to break it.'

'Who'd do that?' asked Suzie.

Lenny lifted a shoulder. 'Who knows? Kids sometimes find an exhausted bird and think it's a plaything. There are feathers out of his tail as well.'

'Can we still race him?' I asked.

'Not this season,' Lenny replied. He needs time to recover now. It's disappointing, he was coming on well. It's a puzzle – still, that's pigeons for you.'

As he finished, a door banged to in the house and a gruff voice shouted, 'Dad? Where are you?'

Warren. I noticed Suzie tense. Within seconds, he was striding up the garden towards us. I could see the confusion in his untanned face long before he halted by the corner of the loft.

Lenny reached for his wallet. 'How much do you want?'

Warren didn't even look at his dad. He glared briefly at Suzie, even less at me. His dark eyes fell on Pawnee Warrior. 'Forget it,' he growled. 'Gotta be somewhere.' He walked backwards a pace then turned and swept away, whacking a fist into the nearest piece of hedge.

Lenny shook his head in deep despair. 'Put the bird in. I need to sort this out.' He sighed and went after Warren.

As soon as he'd gone, Suzie whispered, 'What do you reckon?'

I thought it was obvious. Warren didn't like the fact that Pawnee was back. His hold over me had slipped again. But why would that make him storm away? With so much pent-up anger inside him? As if someone had kicked him while he was down? I ran the scene over, trying to find a reason. Nothing would come, but

245

one thing did stick in my mind: the words he'd used when he'd turned away. *Gotta be somewhere*.

Gotta be somewhere.

It was just the sort of thing Susan Duckins might have said.

CHAPTER THIRTY-FIVE

Garry reacted like we'd won the cup.

'*Champi-uns,*' he sang, his voice reaching out across the whole park. He kicked a twig into the middle of the bowling green. Two old dodderers, dressed in white flannels, gawped skywards as if the culprits were aliens. We scarpered before they could give us any grief.

'Bet Warren was totally cheesed,' he said. 'Bet he thought Pawnee had been mangled by falcons and that you'd go and jump off a cliff or something.'

'*Thanks*, Gazza.'

A dumb grin lit up his lightly-tanned face.

It felt good to have him back. Although I hadn't seen him for absolutely ages, it was just as if we'd never really been apart. He hadn't once made me crawl for bagging him off. And when I told him all the stuff that had happened at the funeral, and Pawnee going missing on top, like Suzie, he'd just been dead supportive.

'It's brill that you've got him back,' he said.

I nodded and bounced a football on the path. 'Gotta be careful, though. I don't trust Warren. He looked dead crazed.'

'Nah, he's stuffed,' said Garry. '*Champi-uns!*' He whacked the ball high into the air.

Tennis courts this time.

Nice shot, Gazza.

Despite Garry's confidence, I really did have the feeling that Warren might retaliate. I'd been to Barrowmoor three times since Pawnee's return, just to check he was there – and OK. I made the excuse to Mr Spigott that there was nothing much to do in the summer holidays and, if he didn't mind me coming, I could help midweek with his race returns, as well as basketing up on Fridays – plus any other jobs he had around the loft.

One day he asked, was I good with computers? Before I knew it, he had me typing in records of race times for the youngsters. He showed me how to calculate a bird's velocity. 'People who know nowt about flying pigeons think the winner of a race is the bird that homes first, which is a bit unfair when you consider that the lofts are all set at different distances from the liberation points. Alf's, for instance, was two miles further south than mine. So the winner is the bird that flies the fastest, in yards per minute. Divide the distance flown by the time recorded and you've got it. Got it?'

Just about. Mr Anwar would have been proud. Formulas, spreadsheets, multi-coloured graphs. Better than any of our IT projects. Once I'd got the hang of it I plotted lots of graphs, so Lenny could easily see which young birds were improving the most.

'Why do you want to know?' I asked.

He clicked on another program. A blank race sheet appeared on the screen. In the box marked RACE POINT, he typed 'Picauville'. 'Town in Northern France,' he said. 'Nice race for a fit young bird. Two hundred and fifty miles, cross Channel. Good prize money, too. I'll be looking to send our best dozen youngsters. We need to start making decisions now because—'

He broke off as the front door slammed. Warren oozed in and flopped into a chair. 'Don't mind me, I just live here,' he sneered.

Lenny stayed cool. 'There's some chicken in the fridge. Make yourself useful and do us both a wedge.' He turned to me again. 'Picauville's a week on Saturday. If you were thinking of coming to basket them up, it's Thursday night, not Friday, for long-distance races, because of the extra travel involved.'

'Picauville,' said Warren, clicking his tongue. 'Haven't won that for a few years, Dad.' He kicked off his boots and rose to his feet. 'Maybe Darryl will bring you luck. He might even make a sarnie if you ask him nicely.' He sneered again and disappeared upstairs.

'Ignore him,' said Lenny, seeing me tense. 'Work on those graphs and find me twelve good 'uns. Maybe he's right. Maybe we will get lucky this year. By the way, if you do intend coming over next weekend, the routine will be slightly different. I'm away exhibiting some paintings on the Friday. I'll be leaving Thursday night, after I've taken the birds to the club. I won't be flying any inland races 'cos I won't be back here till Saturday lunch. I'll be coming from your direction. Pick you up, if you like?'

'OK,' I said. 'Oh, I remembered, you wanted this.' I handed him a scrap of paper.

'Comanche Princess and Chocolate what?'

'Ridge,' I said. 'Choctaw Ridge. It's an Indian name.'

'Aye, I thought as much,' he said. 'Crikey, the

rate you're going, we'll have a tepee instead of a loft before long.'

The days rolled by. Thursday came and everything was cool. When I arrived at Station Road, Lenny was busy parcelling up a painting. By now, we'd chosen our birds for Picauville. All I had to do was basket them up, then remind Lenny to sign the race sheet. As usual, he'd left this till the very last minute – in case any bird was ill and another needed to be sent in its place.

'Any problems, leave me a note,' he said. 'I'm glad you've come over, 'cos I'm pushed for time – and I must have a word with Warren before he goes.'

'Goes?' I said.

Lenny pointed at the ceiling. 'Upstairs, packing. Announced last night he was off to some festival with his mates. Four days there, then they're slumming it round Europe. Reckons he'll be gone three months at least.'

Three months. No Warren. My spirits soared. Maybe he'd tired of torturing me at last.

'Go on, look lively,' Lenny said. He ushered me to the garden as the telephone rang. 'When you're finished, leave the baskets just inside the garage. Cocks and hens in separate ones, remember. See you lunchtime, Saturday, if I miss you tonight.'

He hurried to the phone.

I hurried to the loft.

The birds were all in top condition. Only one, a mealy cock, had dropped a flight. I didn't think it was enough to have it scratched from the race, but Lenny would have to decide. I made a note of its number and put it in the basket.

Before I left, I held Pawnee. He looked brilliant. The gash in his leg had healed. His eye was lively, his feathers gleaming. He felt firm and buoyant in my hands. 'One day, you'll win a race like this,' I whispered, then kissed his speckled head and put him back on his perch.

I buckled up the basket and took it to the garage, then went into the house in search of Lenny.

Warren was sitting in the kitchen. 'He's in the shower,' he said as I scanned the lounge. 'Sit down, Darryl. Fancy a beer?' He took a swig from a can of lager, then slammed it on the table and slid it towards me.

More games. I wasn't going to stay near him. 'Tell your dad to look at the mealy, please. It's number ten on the sheet.'

He yawned.

I sighed and picked up a pencil.

'Leave it,' he snarled. 'Ten. I'll tell him.'

I left a note anyway. 'Have a nice holiday,' I said.

And beat it before he spat his drink in my face.

Mr Spigott picked me up on the Saturday as promised. We put my bike in the back of his car. I told him I was planning to ride on to Suzie's as soon as we'd clocked the young birds in. 'When will they start arriving?' I asked.

'Depends on the weather,' he said a bit tautly. 'I listened to the forecast on the way up. There's a strong north-easterly wind across the Channel. That'll slow them down a bit. Never mind, eh? You can fill the time doing your usual jobs.'

Whoopee. Two hours of scraping. Thanks.

But it didn't work out like that. The whole complexion of the afternoon changed the moment we turned down Station Road. A bike was lying on Lenny's drive.

'For Pete's sake, who's left that there?' he chuntered, having to pull up in the street.

We looked towards the house. A forlorn figure was sitting on the step.

It was Susan Duckins.

She was full of tears.

253

CHAPTER THIRTY-SIX

Lenny switched off the engine and unclipped his seatbelt. 'Do you know owt about this?'

'No,' I said. 'I haven't seen her for ages.'

He frowned in confusion and got out of the car.

I followed him up the drive, a strange anxiety rising in my throat. Susan, by now, had her head bent low, brown hair lapping around her knees. The sleeves of her sweater were stretched across her fists. A few waterlogged tissues lay abandoned round her feet.

Lenny leaned over her and opened the door. 'Susan? What's the matter, lass?'

In a muffled sob she said, 'Send Darryl away.'

He took a firm breath. 'I can't do that. Come on, step inside and tell me what's up.' He reached down and helped her stand. She looked awful, like a pan that had just boiled over. Streaks of mascara were running down her cheeks, merging with smudges of strawberry-coloured lipstick. Her eyes were lost behind a veil of tears. She must have been crying for hours.

Lenny sat her on the sofa with a box of tissues. The house was quiet, no sign of Warren. Had she come here looking for him? That was Lenny's opening question.

'He hates me,' she sobbed, pushing the heel of a palm across her cheeks.

'What's he done?' said Lenny, searching for his fags.

She pulled a tissue through her hands. 'Darryl's still here.'

'So?' I snapped.

Lenny shushed me and said, 'Go and see to the birds.'

'But—?'

He flicked a hand. 'Go on.'

I muttered a swear word under my breath and started to move towards the garden. But I'd hardly turned my back when Susan blurted, 'Is he all right? The bird? Darryl's chequer?'

She meant Pawnee. I swung round. 'What?'

Lenny stopped me with a hand. 'What are you saying, Susan?'

'I know it came back,' she gabbled, a rogue

tear spilling over her lid. 'I tried to kid him they'd escaped from the shed, but he didn't believe me. He hit me *so* hard.'

She collapsed on her side and we both saw the shadow of a bruise below her ear. Lenny's mood immediately darkened. He fumbled with his cigarettes and brought one to his mouth, cursing when it bounced off his trembling lip. He tossed them aside. 'Hit you? When? When did this happen?'

Susan hugged a cushion. 'I can't remember. About . . . two weeks, I think.'

'That was when the birds went missing,' I said.

Lenny rubbed a hand across his cheek. 'Are you telling us that Warren snatched Darryl's bird – before I got home from the training toss?'

Susan nodded, pulling strands of hair from her mouth. 'I was here, in the garden, when they came in. He took three, so it wouldn't look too suspicious. He said it was a joke to wind Darryl up. I said we shouldn't, because it was cruel. But he kept on saying that Darryl deserved it. He said Darryl was an insult to the memory of his mum. He was always going on about his mum. It scared me, Mr Spigott. He got so *angry* when he talked about her.' She beat a fist softly on the arm of the sofa, screwing up her eyes so she wouldn't cry again.

Lenny crouched down and steadied her hand. 'How did Pawnee end up in Derby?'

'I rescued him,' she sniffed. 'I took him away. Warren had them in a box – in a shed, on Ginger's dad's allotment.'

'What? Why didn't you tell me?' I stormed.

'I *tried*,' she bawled. 'I went to your house. Your stupid dad wouldn't let me in.'

'She's lying,' I said to Lenny. 'Dad never said anything about her coming.'

'Well, he wouldn't!' she screamed, sitting up and trying to kick me. 'He's useless, just like you!'

'Hey, hey,' said Lenny, keeping us apart. 'There's nothing to be gained from you pair scrapping.'

She sank against his shoulder, pouring out the pain. 'I was so frightened after Warren killed the first bird.'

Lenny gave a tight-lipped nod. 'He reported it to Cheltenham, didn't he?'

'Yes,' she said, making hiccupping noises. 'He told them he'd found it dead in a field and said it looked like another bird had got it. But it *hadn't*. He wrung its neck in front of me one day. He was annoyed because you hadn't tried to contact Darryl. He said he would give you another two days, then he'd do the next one. He was going to pluck it and roast it and feed it to you, so you'd think it was chicken . . .'

I clamped a hand to my mouth as my stomach retched.

'I was going to tell Darryl's dad, honest,' she repeated. 'But he just wouldn't listen. He said I'd hurt Darryl enough and I wasn't to call round or ring him again. He wouldn't tell Darryl I'd been there, either. So I went to the allotments and I got the birds myself. My mum was going to see my auntie, in Bolton, to take her some things from Grandad's will. I asked her to release the birds when she got there. I told her I was helping someone to train them.'

'Was it you who cut the ring?'

'Yes,' she admitted.

'Why?' I shouted. 'He could have been lost for ever.'

'Well, what did you *want*?' she yelled, a trail of snot running over her lip. 'I was trying to save him from Warren!'

Lenny gripped her by the shoulders and turned her to him. 'Why didn't you just come to me?'

'I couldn't,' she whispered, wiping her mouth. 'He would have found out and finished with me.' Her gaze slipped away into deep, soft focus.

'I loved him,' she said in a whiny little voice. 'I'm so sorry.'

'You're not sorry for anything,' I snapped. 'You were there when Sioux died. You killed her, didn't you? You killed a baby bird because you *loved* Warren.'

'What?' she said, shaking her head.

'Darryl, that's enough,' Lenny said angrily.

Susan looked at him, dazed and pleading. 'I didn't kill anything, Mr Spigott. Please, I wouldn't hurt a squab.'

'I know,' he said, thumbing her shoulder. 'The squab died of natural causes. No-one's to blame. No-one. Understood?' He was telling us both, but glaring at me. He turned and spoke softly to Susan again. 'Why did Warren hit you – because you tried to help Pawnee?'

She closed her eyes and nodded. 'He called me a stupid cow and told me to stay out of his plans in future. And I was going to. I was. Until I found out . . .'

'What?' I said. 'What else has he done?'

She lowered her head and played with a tissue. 'It's personal,' she sobbed. She glanced up at Lenny.

His thin grey eyebrows creased in thought. 'Darryl,' he said, 'go and open the lofts.'

'Why? What's she talking about?'

'Please, son, just go and do your jobs. I need to talk to Susan in private.'

He wouldn't look at me, then, but I knew he was serious. I stormed up the garden, my head full of rage. Why was it me who was being 'red-carded'? Why was he taking Susan's side? What could be more 'personal' than the lies she'd told or the things she'd done to help Warren get Pawnee?

I slid the loft doors open and grabbed my scraper. The young birds that hadn't been entered for Picauville fluttered anxiously around their perches. One of them landed on the floor in front of me: the mealy I'd marked on the race sheet. So Lenny had only sent eleven to France – but that should have meant nine birds in the loft. I could only see eight.

Pawnee Warrior wasn't among them.

I hurtled down the garden and burst into the house. Mr Spigott was about to pick up the phone. 'What's the matter?' he said. 'This is important.'

'Pawnee's gone! He's not in the loft.'

'Gone? What are you talking about?'

'He's not *there*. Didn't you see when you put the mealy back?'

Lenny shook his head. 'I haven't touched

a mealy. You left no message on Thursday night, so I took the baskets, as they were, to the club.'

'*Where is he?!*' I screamed, storming over to Susan. 'What's Warren done with him? Where's my bird?!'

'Don't hit me,' she wailed, tightening up.

'Darryl, let her be.' Lenny hauled me back. 'How many young are in the loft?'

I staggered to the hall door, slamming my fists. 'Eight,' I breathed. 'Warren's taken him.'

Lenny glanced across the room. 'He can't have done. There's no message on the answerphone. The club secretary would have called if we'd been a bird short. That means twelve were on the transporter.'

'What—?'

Lenny read my eyes. 'Aye,' he said as we worked it out together. 'Your bird's gone to France in place of the mealy. The swine must have switched them on Thursday night, while I was still in the shower. He must have reprinted the race sheet, too.'

'Didn't you look at it?' I cried.

Lenny pressed his brow. 'I just signed it, lad. I had no reason to think it was amiss.'

'But Pawnee's too young for a race like that. And what about the winds across the Channel?

What if Warren's pulled his flights or poisoned him or—?'

Lenny opened his hands in a helpless gesture. 'Darryl, those birds were released at seven this morning. There's nothing I can do to change that now. The best you can do is wait by the loft and hope by some miracle yours comes in. He's strong, a born racer. I can't offer you any more comfort than that. I'll deal with Warren when the time is right. But my main task now is to get this lass home.' He took off his coat and draped it round her. 'I'm popping to the bathroom, then we're off, OK?'

She nodded in thanks. Lenny swept upstairs.

As soon as he'd gone, I turned on her again. 'Where is he?'

'Who?'

'Warren, stupid.'

'How should I know?' she said. She cowered away, scared.

'You *must* know how to find him.'

'I'll call Mr Spigott if you touch me,' she said.

'Tell me where he is.'

'I don't *know*, OK? I thought he'd be here.'

'Liar. He's going away with his mates.'

'Not until tonight. He told me yesterday. He's dumped me. He won't answer any of my messages.' She fiddled in her pocket for her mobile phone, bipped a few buttons, then bounced it on the sofa.

That was when I had the idea. 'Send him a message from me,' I said coldly.

Her face screwed into a frown. 'Get lost.'

I dived forward and snatched up the phone.

'Hey! Gimme that back.'

She made a half-hearted swipe, but I skipped away, holding the phone up high like a trophy. 'I'm gonna call him out – to the graveyard.'

'You?' she sneered, looping her hair. 'You, fight Warren? He'll tear you to bits. Go on, then, big mouth. Send your message.'

No. Not yet. I dropped the phone into my pocket and waved goodbye.

'What're you doing?' she gasped. Her eyes tracked me to the door.

Simple. I didn't know how to send a message – but one of my angels would. 'Gotta go,' I said. *'Gotta be somewhere.'*

'Darryl, you can't take my *phone*!'

Oh no? Try and stop me, Duck Egg. I had friends to find, a trap to set.

It wasn't over.

Now it was war.

CHAPTER THIRTY-SEVEN

I lay in wait at the corner of the church, hidden in the shadows of a slime-covered buttress. It smelt of dog pee and badly-blocked drains, but it gave me a view of the path from the road and a clear sight of Emily Spigott's grave.

Warren arrived right on cue. He came the way Lenny and I had done when we'd brought Pawnee on his training toss. He was dressed from head to toe in black, all except for the cream-coloured T-shirt he was wearing underneath his loose-fitting jacket and the silver name bracelet tagged around his wrist.

I pressed tight against the wall as he swung past the church. He carried on down towards the oak, dead twigs cracking under his heels. As he dipped into the shade I fell in behind him, creeping quietly between the graves.

He called her name. It died among the trees.

He called again. Only birds replied.

With a buzz of irritation, he propped himself against his mother's headstone and pushed half a cigarette between his lips. I waited for the jet of flame from the lighter, then I made my whoop.

Woo-oo-oo-oo-ooh!

He swore and the lighter danced in his hands. As he jumped to avoid the flame, the heel of his boot caught a smooth-sided stone. He stumbled backwards, almost going over.

I came out of hiding and walked towards him, stopping several metres away. At first I thought he would never see me. But, in some ways, that was part of the plan. While I'd been waiting, my mind had been focused, not on the coming confrontation, but on one of Mr Preston's science lessons. The one about the survival of the fittest: how to confuse or frighten your predator with camouflage or fearsome displays of colour.

The war paint was barely dry on my face, the gel still setting in my hair, the feathers rustling at the back of my neck. I had a red wolf's head on the front of my T-shirt.

I was Pawnee.

'You?' sneered Warren. 'What are you doing here?' He looked me up and down.

I stood and stared.

'Where's Susan?' he snarled, glancing about.

I lobbed her mobile onto the grass. He watched it tumble into the weeds. 'Where is she, you toe-rag?' He flicked the fag away and took a step forward.

'She's with your dad,' I said.

That rattled him, made him freeze, just like the angels had predicted it would. We'd met, all four of us, at Suzie's house and had a 'powwow', of sorts, about Warren and the Duck Egg. The girls had spent ages whispering together, discussing what sort of message we should send. Garry's suggestion had sounded good to me: 'Come – if you think you're hard enough'. But the girls had quickly tutted that one aside and Gemma had texted something 'subtle': 'Darryl KNOWS. Graveyard in 1. Got 2 talk. S. xx'

'Knows what?' I'd asked, but they wouldn't say.

Who cared? The snake was here.

'I know what you did with my bird,' I breathed.

'Your bird,' he spat. Now he had the crazed look in his eyes. 'That cock was bred from one of mine. It came from Little Elf. *I* decide where Little Elf flies. You wanna be me? You wanna *take my place*?' He kicked a pot of flowers off his mother's grave, then stood on the mound with his arms stretched wide. 'Well, come on, Geronimo, knock me off.'

I stood and stared. 'Pawnee's *my* bird. And now you're gonna pay.'

He touched his fingers to his chest. 'Me? You're gonna make *me* pay?' He stepped off the grave and swaggered towards me. 'You cocky little toe-rag. I'm gonna shove those feathers right up your—'

Woo-oo-oo-oo-ooh! The second war whoop came from behind him.

He whipped around. Suzie was ghosting through the graves. Like me, her face was splashed with colour.

Warren laughed and gave a scornful clap. 'Nice one, Darryl. Brought your *squaw*?'

'Two,' I said.

Woo-oo-oo-oo-ooh! Gemma appeared from the bushes to his left.

Woo-oo-oo-oo-ooh! Garry from his right.

Warren nodded slowly, weighing it up. 'OK, hero. Let's do it.'

I put my head down, and charged.

I hit him in the midriff, but couldn't take him over. His fist came down like a hammer on my ear. Before the pain had truly burned in, his right knee came up under my jaw. My teeth snapped together with a jarring crack. Dizzied, I stumbled against a headstone. A spray of flowers, in their cellophane, broke my fall. Gemma was on his back by then, tugging at his hair as if the top of his skull would open like a trapdoor. Warren swore, bent forward and crashed her to the ground. She squealed in pain and clutched her arm. Warren spat at her face and swung his boot, forgetting that Garry was just within range. Garry let fly with a kick of his own. He missed Warren's shin and thudded instead into the muscles of his calf. Warren swore even louder and flung out an arm. Garry ducked just in time, the blow skimming his head by the thickness of his dandruff. Then, stupidly, he straightened up and flapped a punch. Too slow. Too weak. In a flash, Warren had a fistful of jumper. He yanked Garry forward and tupped him, hard. The bridge of Garry's nose took the force of the head butt. He bounced back, both hands clutching his face: blood was seeping through the web of his fingers.

Then it was Suzie's turn.

'Oi!' she shouted.

Warren turned to face her.

'Nice boots,' she snarled. 'Make you look taller.'

Warren stepped forward and aimed a punch. He was staring at the sky before he knew it.

She held him like she'd once held me, locking his arm straight, threatening to break it. She pressed a foot into his armpit. His jacket sleeve ripped. Warren squirmed in pain and called her every murderous name he could think of. 'Darryl, get his other arm,' she shouted.

I leapt onto his chest and pinned him with my knees. Gemma, the only one of the five of us in tears, called him a loud-mouthed pig and tried to shove a fistful of grass between his teeth. Warren tried to bite her. She slapped his face.

Gazza moved in, blood dripping from his nose. He dived on Warren's legs, fixing his ankles.

'Boots off,' said Gemma and blew Warren a kiss.

'You're gonna die,' he spat. 'You're all gonna *die*.'

Then I showed him the scissors.

His body arched.

'Keep him down,' cried Suzie, tightening her grip.

Warren barked in pain and gave her one of those long dark looks, recording her face for the next time we met. If there was a next time.

I grabbed a fistful of his hair and tugged him round. 'You're gonna pay,' I breathed.

'I'll kill every bird you ever had, Otterwell.'

'Darryl, just do it,' Suzie snapped.

Warren's eyes flicked from her to the scissors. I felt him kick.

'We've got his boots,' said Garry.

'Ugh,' went Gemma. 'His feet *stink*.'

Suzie nudged me with her kneecap. 'Scalp him, then we split.'

Warren's eyes seemed to fill the whole of his face. 'Touch me and I'll never let you go you little—'

I clicked the scissors sharply, cutting him off, then moved them close to the ridge of his brow. 'This is for Pawnee and Sioux,' I said. I whooped in a whisper. Then I went in.

He screamed as I worked the blades. I made sure they were pressing down against his skull so every snip would reverberate through his brain. I went for the sides, where the hair was longest. It was sleek, unwashed. It came away with ease. As my hold on him loosened, he tossed his head and the last few strands ripped out from their roots. He roared in pain. The back of his head hit the hard brown earth. He panted, squealing that his arm was broken. 'I'd know,' said Suzie, and held on tight.

I sat back and showed him a huge lock of hair.

'Give it here,' urged Gemma. 'I'll stuff it in his boots. C'mon, Darryl. Garry's hurt.'

But Warren and I were in a face-off now. I was staring deep into the pools of his soul. I saw his spirit, fading away. My fist tightened around my coup. I had my medicine. The symbol of his power. With it, he could never hurt me again. 'I'm keeping it,' I said, and held the hair high.

'You'll wish you were never born,' he hissed.

The war paint creased around my eyes. I looked at my hands. Scissors in one fist, hair in the other. I brought them together, predator and prey. The scissors flipped over, points aimed down.

'What are you doing?' panted Suzie, shortening her stance. 'I can't hold him much longer.' There was fear in her voice.

There was more in Warren's. 'Get him off me!' he squealed.

I clamped the scissors – tight, like a dagger.

Warren's body began to quake.

'Darryl!' shouted Suzie. 'What are you *doing*?'

Somewhere up ahead I heard tyres on gravel.

'Feds!' cried Gemma.

Garry loosened his hold. Warren bucked and his legs went into spasm.

Car doors opened. A voice thick with authority called: 'Police. Stop what you're doing and stay where you are.'

I raised the scissors.

'Nooo!' screamed Warren.

'Darryl!' yelled Suzie. She let go of Warren and kicked me in the ribs, a punching kick with the flat of her foot.

I fell sideways. The scissors ploughed into the earth.

Warren rolled over, got up, ran.

'Warren?' yelled another voice: Lenny Spigott. He went pounding through the churchyard after his son.

One of the two policemen gave chase. The other, a tubby, balding man, pointed a commanding finger and barked: 'You lot: Hiawatha's tribe, stay put.' He spoke into his radio. 'One five seven to Charlie Echo. Suspect running through St Barnabas' churchyard, heading for the rail— Oi, you! Get back here!'

Too late. I was on my way.

I scrabbled to the top of the railway embankment in time to see Warren slithering to the bottom. The second copper collared me and held me back. Lenny Spigott was stepping down as fast as he could, all the time calling, 'Warren, wait!'

Warren hit the side of the railway track and carried on running, parallel to the line. In the distance, a train appeared. Not a slow-moving goods train; the bright yellow nose of an Inter-City engine.

'Warren!' screamed Lenny.

Chest heaving, Warren turned to look for his pursuers. He stumbled backwards onto the line.

'WAR-RENNNN!' screamed Lenny. *'Warren, no!'*

Then the train flashed past.

And Warren was gone.

CHAPTER THIRTY-EIGHT

They called another panda, took Garry to the hospital and the three of us to Barrowmoor police station. From there, they rang our parents. Dad arrived on a screech of tyres; Mr McAllister five minutes later. Gemma's mother turned up in blue sunglasses, as if she didn't want to be identified.

They spoke to me and Dad on our own for ages, then gathered us together in an interview room. After what seemed like the whole weekend, a man called Sergeant Palmer came in. He was about Dad's age, tall, red-haired with ginger freckles. He dropped a folder on the desk and sat down quietly, jiggling the knot of his dark blue tie.

'I've seen a lot of villains in this room,' he said, 'muggers, flashers, dealers, drunks. I have never met the three little Indians before – correction, four little Indians. Your companion, Garry Taylor, has a broken nose and a face like a winning football coupon: eight stitches, all in a line.'

Mrs Thomson cleared her throat. 'How long will the children have to stay in custody?'

Sergeant Palmer creaked back in his chair. 'The "children" have not been arrested, madam.'

Suzie, sitting beside me, shuddered.

'Are you charging them with anything?' her father asked.

Sergeant Palmer opened a drawer and took out a large, clear polythene bag. He laid it on the desk. In the bag were Suzie's scissors. 'I'd like to clarify what these were for.'

'His hair,' Gemma burbled. 'They were just to cut his hair.' Her glance found me. I switched my gaze to the floor.

With one finger, Sergeant Palmer flicked the folder open. 'Let me read you something. This is from the statement of PC Steele, one of the officers at the scene. *As I stepped out of the car it was clear that a scuffle was taking place. All five youths appeared to be involved. The boy, Otterwell, identified by the wolf on his T-shirt, was kneeling on the youth I now know to be Spigott. I saw a glint of light as though from a blade. I formed the opinion that Otterwell might have possessed a knife.'*

Dad breathed in slowly. I kept my head down.

'The girl, Thomson, on seeing the patrol car, stood up and ran to the front of the group, thus obscuring my view of the fight. I called a warning. I heard a voice shout "No". The girl, McAllister, who was holding Spigott in some sort of arm lock, shouted to Otterwell by name, "Darryl!" It seemed to me she was attempting to dissuade him from going through with some sort of act. She kicked him aside, letting Spigott escape. On arrival at the scene, I found a pair of scissors implanted in the earth. They had been forced in by a stabbing motion . . .'

Sergeant Palmer closed the file. 'Look at me. All three of you.' He pointed to the scissors. 'If these had as much as scratched Warren Spigott, then you' – he levelled a finger at me – 'would be looking at a charge of wounding, or grievous bodily harm, or attempted murder—'

'Oh my God,' said Mrs Thomson.

'—or worse.'

Suzie burst into tears. Mr McAllister gave her a hug. 'Do you have to be so brutal?'

Sergeant Palmer turned a pencil through his fingers. 'Warren Spigott, were he here, might have asked the same thing.'

'Spigott's a thug,' said Dad.

Sergeant Palmer shrugged, unimpressed.

'But what about everything he's done to Darryl?!' Gemma flung out a furious hand.

The sergeant checked his notes. 'As far as I can ascertain, all Spigott has "done" is fail to pass on a telephone message, kiss his girlfriend in public and hide a pigeon in a box on an allotment. A judge and jury will not regard that as sufficient vindication for what could have been a fatal attack.'

'He sent Pawnee to France,' I cried.

'Spigott's been torturing him for months,' said Dad.

Sergeant Palmer nodded briefly. 'That may be so. But your son has to learn that *we* administer the law, Mr Otterwell, not him. As for Spigott swapping those birds, there's no direct evidence to prove that he did.'

'Well, who else could have done it?' I said.

The sergeant swung idly in his chair. 'An inventive barrister could easily suggest you set the whole thing up to persuade your friends to help you seek revenge on Spigott, Darryl.'

'That's ridiculous,' snapped Dad.

Suzie cried and cried. Mr McAllister eyed me suspiciously.

Dad ran a tired hand through his hair. 'This is outrageous. You came to *arrest* Spigott. PC Steele – he told me so himself.'

'Why did you want him?' Mrs Thomson asked.

Sergeant Palmer rolled the pencil under his fingers. 'We were anxious to speak to Warren Spigott in connection with another criminal matter. I'm not at liberty to say what it was.'

'Is it because he hit Susan?' I asked.

The sergeant said, 'I can't answer that.'

Dad slapped his hands down onto his thighs. 'Well, is that it?'

'Yes – for now.'

'For now?' Mrs Thomson gripped Gemma's hand.

Sergeant Palmer gathered up his notes. 'If Warren Spigott files a complaint, I will have to speak to all of you again.'

'He's not dead, then?' said Gemma, wrinkling her nose.

The sergeant dropped the pencil into his pocket. 'He's not splattered all over the three-thirty to Sheffield, if that's what you mean. He's given us the slip. We'll find him soon enough. He won't get far without his boots.' He smirked, and tilted his head towards the door.

Mr McAllister ushered Suzie to her feet. At the door she half-turned and looked over her shoulder. Her tear-stained eyes were full of pain. I guessed this was going to be the last time I'd see her – for a while, at least. Her dad bundled her away before I could speak. Gemma and her mum followed on behind.

Sergeant Palmer pressed a small card into my hand. 'That's my mobile number. Keep it with you, everywhere you go. If Spigott tries anything, call me at once. No more daft heroics, OK?'

I nodded and made a fist in my pocket. Who needed heroics?

I had Warren's soul . . .

'. . . his *soul*? How?' scoffed Garry.

'By scalping him, stupid.' I tutted and told him to pass me a pin. We were in my new room, putting posters on the wall, trying to hide the glare of fresh blue paint. We'd both been grounded for the past two weeks. Sometimes, I wished it could have been four. 'If you take someone's hair, it gives you powerful medicine over them. Honestly, you'll never make a flipping warrior.'

He handed me the pin. 'I don't wanna be a warrior; I wanna be a striker. And if you ask me, Warren's gonna want his hair back – or have *yours* instead. Have you really kept it or are you just dissing me?'

I looked at him straight. 'Do you swear on the

spirits of your dead ancestors never to reveal the sacred site?'

He screwed up his nose and immediately went 'Ow'. His stitches had only been out a few days. Some nasal moves were still off-limits. 'Sacred what?'

'Swear, first.'

'Sausages.'

'Oh, fun-nee.' I reached under the bed and brought out a shoe-box. I let him peek inside.

'Is that it, a bit of blue cloth?'

'Gazza, this is my medicine bundle. The start of it, anyway. All braves have these. This is how I'm keeping Warren away.' I lifted a fold. A piece of jet-black hair poked out. 'When Pawnee comes home, I'm gonna add one of his feathers to the bundle. That'll really do it. Warren'll be cooked.'

Garry sat back, chewing his thumb. 'It's been ages, though. How do you know he's not . . . y'know?'

Dead? No way. 'The medicine will guide him to safety,' I said. 'The weather was bad for the Picauville race that day. Lenny lost four birds, but they weren't protected like Pawnee.' I glanced through the window, north to Barrowmoor. 'When he comes home, I'm going to go and see him. I'll use the medicine if I have to, to make Mum agree. I'm going back properly next year, anyway, when we start training Comanche and Choctaw. Mum will have had the twins by then. She'll be dead mumsy, easy to persuade.'

'Babies,' said Garry, making a face. 'It's gonna be scary, coming here. Your stupid sister's bad enough.'

'Nat's cool,' I said. 'She makes me things.'

'She do this?' He picked something off the floor: a small red heart with a D inside it.

'Gazza, give me that, please.'

'Aw, no,' he groaned. 'It's not from *her*? She's not sent you *another* letter?'

'Five, if you must know. Give me that heart.'

'Can I read one?' he said, handing it over.

'No. Stuff off.'

'Why? Does she scrawl, "I love you, Darryl" over and over in different directions and loads of colours?'

'No,' I said tautly (well, not since the first one).

'You've gone dead soft on her,' he said. 'Bet you've got a calendar with crossed-off days. I bet you're all piney for the holidays to end 'cos her dad can't stop her seeing you at school.'

'Yeah, well, *you* just wanna get back so you can snog Gemma Thomson.'

His face turned the colour of the heart he'd found. 'She only came round to nurse me once.'

Nurse him? I grinned and his ears lit up. He had the look of a boy who'd said too much.

A knock on the door spared him a grilling. 'Darryl?' It was Mum's voice.

'Yeah?'

'There's a call.'

'Is it Gran?' She was due to ring today. She'd been ringing me a lot just lately.

Mum opened the door. Her face was drawn. 'No, it's Mr Spigott – he's got news of Pawnee.'

I worked the medicine straight away on Dad. One strand of hair, pressed onto his arm. Please would he take us to Station Road?

He raised an eyebrow at Mum, and picked up his keys.

I hadn't seen Lenny since the day we'd jumped Warren. But he was civil, as always, almost happy. In the lounge he shook hands with Dad, clapped my shoulder and said hello to Garry.

Before I could ask about Pawnee, the toilet flushed and feet came clomping down the stairs. Someone else was in the house. I touched the hair in my pocket as the lounge door opened.

To my astonishment, in walked Susan Duckins. She flounced across the room and sank into a chair. 'Darryl,' she said, with her usual huff, 'why are you *always* gawping at me?'

'What's *she* doing here?' asked Garry.

Lenny stuck out his chin. I thought this must be a cigarette moment, but the pack stayed firmly in his pocket. 'Susan is welcome to visit whenever she likes.'

'How come?' said Garry, subtle as ever.

'It's none of your *business*,' Susan sniped.

'All right, lass.' Lenny gestured for calm. Then, in a measured voice he said, 'Warren . . . hurt Susan very badly. I feel it's my duty to offer my support.' His gaze immediately locked with Dad's. I'd seen this before. Secret adult code. Telepathic bonding. Even the medicine couldn't break it. Not that I cared. Susan Duckins was history.

'Is there any news of Warren?' asked Dad. His eyes flickered briefly over Susan.

'On the continent,' said Lenny, a twist of irony in his voice. 'Got through the tunnel – into France. Can't see him coming back. If he does, he'll be stopped and he'll have to face the music.'

'Gone?' said Garry. He clenched a fist in triumph.

I didn't make a move, but my mind was crying, *Yes*.

Lenny reached down and touched Susan's shoulder. 'Tell Darryl what he really wants to hear.'

Her doe eyes rolled up, beautiful, filming. 'Pawnee Warrior came home,' she said.

'Come on,' said Lenny. 'Let's go and see him.'

At first glance, he looked no different from usual. But when Lenny started fanning his wings and tail, it soon became clear how much he'd been through. Several feathers were shattered or lost and the dark green stains around his vent were a sign, I knew, of bacterial infection. But Lenny's mood was bright. 'He's led a charmed life, this bird,' he said. 'But he's a battler; there's no denying his spirit. By all the laws of pigeon racing he should have been feet up, floating in the Channel. Somehow, he found his way home. That's the sort of bird I want in my loft: one with plenty of grit in his crop. But he isn't mine to own – and after all that's happened, I'm not sure it's right for me to keep him here. So if you want him, lad, he's yours to take back.' He put Pawnee into my open hands.

I held him, as Lenny had shown me so often, looking for that special sign in his eye. That glint that would set him apart from other birds. That spark of life which refused to die out. I saw triumph and hope, endurance and courage. I saw Little Elf rising out of the ashes. I glanced at the heart on Lenny's arm and thought about the twins inside my mum. Last of all, I saw me in that tiny copper mirror, and knew there was only one choice I could make.

I returned Pawnee to Mr Spigott.

'Make him a champion,' I said.

THE END

If you enjoyed this book, you might also enjoy reading about how Darryl got his first bird – Cherokee . . .

FLY, CHEROKEE, FLY

by Chris d'Lacey

'You can't kill her,' I stammered, finding my voice. 'Please . . . you can't do that . . .'

Everyone deserves a second chance, even an injured racing pigeon. Darryl, who has always longed for a pet, is determined that Cherokee will fly again. But he doesn't expect that the fight to keep her will mean that he will become a victim himself . . .

'Outstanding' *The Sunday Times*

'Will do for racing pigeons what *Kes* did for birds of prey' *Times Educational Supplement*

0 552 547891

ABOUT THE AUTHOR

Chris d'Lacey was born in Malta in 1954. This makes him a sort of Malteser, which probably explains why he eats so much chocolate. He began writing children's books in 1993. Chris's favourite subjects are animals, aliens, music and football – but not necessarily in that order. He also keeps pigeons.

One day, a long time ago, he found a pigeon with a broken wing. He took it home for 'a few days' to look after it – and ended up keeping it for fourteen years. He called the pigeon Gregory Peck, after the name of a famous actor. It seemed quite funny at the time.

Gregory Peck, the pigeon, died on Christmas Day, 1997. In their fourteen years together, Gregory and his mate Gigi managed to bring several young pigeons into the world, one of whom was known as Cherokee.